PHANTOMS OF THE THEATER

PHANTOMS OF THE THEATER

Raymond Lamont Brown

THOMAS NELSON INC., PUBLISHERS

Nashville   New York

First edition

Library of Congress Cataloging in Publication Data

Brown, Raymond Lamont.
  Phantoms of the theater.

  Bibliography: p.
  1. Ghosts—United States. 2. Ghosts—Europe. 3. Performing arts—United States—Miscellanea. 4. Performing arts—Europe—Miscellanea. I. Title.
BF1472.U6B76   133.1   76–29609
ISBN 0–8407–6502–9

For Jean Elizabeth
who once did not believe

1938617

Contents

PHANTOMS OF THE THEATER

CHAPTER 1

Ghosts
Real and Stage-Managed

Probably the oldest recorded notes on ghosts appear in cuneiform characters on baked clay and date from four thousand years ago. These notes, on twelve tablets found in the ruins of Nineveh (this celebrated ancient city stood on the east bank of the upper River Tigris, opposite modern Mosul, Iraq), tell ''The Babylonian Story of the Flood and the Epic of Gilgamesh''—and give an account of a spirit communication at a séance.

Since then, all ages and all classes of writers have concerned themselves with ghosts, among them Herodotus, Plutarch, and Tertullian. Famous names in English literature, including Daniel Defoe, Dr. Samuel Johnson, Oliver Goldsmith, R. L. Stevenson, and W. B. Yeats, have also reported ghostly activities.

For as long as I can remember, ghosts have fascinated me, and for many years I have been on their trail. I believe in a spirit universe just as real as the world of the living, and aver that, under certain circumstances, each world can overlap the other. It seems to me that ghosts have a great deal to do with the state of mind of the viewer, not in terms of hallucination but in terms of receptivity. Just as animals can have a greater capacity than humans for intuitive psychic cognizance, so I believe that some humans have the talent of seeing ghosts, much as some might have aptitudes for crosswords or nuclear physics.

11

All investigators of psychic phenomena come up against one big drawback: the almost total—as yet—unavailability of ghosts for controlled scientific experiment, coupled with the lack of a proper vocabulary with which to describe logically the activities of ghosts. Dictionaries do not help us to a good definition of what a ghost is, and investigators differ one from another on the same subject. However, the following may be helpful as a rule of thumb for distinguishing the different types of haunting, as taken from the jargon of parapsychology:

Ghost. A spirit body which is a stranger to one who perceives it.

Apparition. A spirit body well known to the percipient (i.e., a relative or friend).

Vision. The spirit body of a prominent religious figure (i.e., a saint).

Poltergeist. A projection of psychic energy that finds its potential through the frustrated creativity of adolescence.

I would be less than honest if I said that I have ever seen a ghost, for I have never seen the materialized spirit body of a person I know to be dead. But I have seen something of what ghosts can do.

One personal experience took place when I lived at Dewsbury, in West Yorkshire. I was invited to take part in a psychic investigation in a house in the neighboring town of Batley. This house had had a number of tenants in rapid succession; none would live there long because of the strange "movements of a chest of drawers."

On my arrival at the house, several photographs were taken with infrared filters. Subsequent development showed no psychic extras. However, when we entered the room deemed haunted, certain things were immediately noticeable to us. Down the wall, behind the chest of drawers, were deep scratch marks to about three feet above the top of the piece of furniture.

After about an hour or so, I and the four other investigators sat in séance and were startled by the creaking of the chest of drawers. Slowly, with a terrible scratching noise, the chest was raised about three feet up the wall. That is how the scratches had been made in the wall.

Investigation showed that the piece of furniture could not have been lifted by mechanical means or by trickery. Its movement was supernatural. Taking the history of the "hauntings" at the house and the movement of this chest of drawers, it was clear that the psychic body here was of poltergeist origin.

The chest of drawers had been present in one of the bedrooms of the house during all its tenancies. It was huge and very heavy, and would have taken four or six hefty men to lift it. It was so large, in fact, that it could not be taken through the door and consequently had been made in the room.

Details of what had happened during the séance were logged and further investigation of the house's history was undertaken.

It appears that around 1900 the house was inhabited by an elderly couple who, from time to time, looked after a seven-year-old grandchild while its parents were out at work. One day the child had been playing in the street when it was killed by a horse and cart. The grandparents were grief stricken.

The child's coffin had rested on the very chest of drawers for three days before it had been buried. Was there an occult connection? It seems likely. Neighbors attested that the "ghostly figure" of the old grandmother had often appeared at the bedroom window looking distraughtly down into the street where the child was killed.

Such cases encouraged me to take a greater interest in ghosts.

Shakespeare's Ghosts

As far as ghosts in plays are concerned, Shakespeare stands head and shoulders above others who write for the theater as a brilliant manipulator of ghostly phenomena. For Shakespeare made his ghosts behave in conformity with the laws that were deemed in his age to govern such phenomena.

The frequency in which Shakespeare used specters shows how widespread was Elizabethan belief in them. Their existence, in fact, was never seriously questioned—people only differed in their evaluation of them. On the one hand, the uneducated saw them as departed spirits of those who had once lived in the flesh and had returned to the mortal plane for revenge and retaliation, retribution, warning, or the guidance of those still living. Scholars, however, were prone to regard ghosts as the manifestation of evil influences not properly understood.

Shakespeare gives us two kinds of ghosts, the objective and the subjective. The objective ghost was purported to be actually present and apparent to several people at the same time. The ghost in *Hamlet* is thus objective. The subjective ghost was recognized as the product of the mind of the person who saw it, a hallucination or fiction of the imagination, as is the ghost of Banquo in *Macbeth* and Caesar's ghost in *Julius Caesar*. Occasionally, of course, ghosts do appear in dreams, as did the apparitions to Richard III before Bosworth Field and to Posthumus in *Cymbeline*. From *Hamlet*, perhaps, we gather the best set of data about popular superstition in Elizabethan times on the subject of ghosts—that is, their appearance in eerie circumstances (dark, silent night); the inability of the specter to speak unless spoken to; rules of return; the terror in the mind of the viewer, and so on.

All in all most writers took their cue from Shakespeare on how to handle stage ghosts. Yet, in the main, ghosts vanished from the stage in the nineteenth century when theatergoers developed a strange liking for more bloody horror.

Pepper's Ghost Effect

Today play producers are going in for many kinds of projection—film projection and slide projection—which can of course be adapted to ghost effects. The time-honored technique of producing fake ghosts on stage involves having a brightly painted gauze stretched tight in front of the "ghost." When lighted from in front, the gauze appears solid and takes on the aspect of a part of the scene. Lighted from behind, any object or person standing there as a ghost suddenly "appears" before the audience's wondering gaze. As the light behind the gauze is taken out, so the ghost disappears!

Undoubtedly the most well-known technique of producing a stage ghost is that of the Pepper's Ghost Effect.

John Henry Pepper, (1821–1900), a chemist, was director and professor of chemistry at the Royal Polytechnic Institution in London. It was he who sponsored scientific experiments into the "ghost effect," originally invented by Henry Dircks in connection with a piece by Charles Dickens.

Here is the original specification of how the ghost works:

> The main purpose, as described in the specification, is, "to associate on the same stage living persons and phantoms to act together." There is a stage like that of a theatre; and an under-stage at a level six feet or so lower, between it and the spectators. The stage can be seen by all the persons in the hall or theatre; but the under-stage (though nearer) is so managed, by means of screens, dimness of light, and dark baize lining, that its existence is scarcely even suspected by most of the spectators. There is a large plate of unsilvered glass nearly upright between the under-stage and the stage, so artfully framed and adjusted as to be invisible, and allowing persons on the stage to be seen almost as clearly as if there were no glass there. An actor, whom we will call the hidden actor, is on the under-stage, entirely below the level of the real stage, and out of the sight of the spectators. A strong light is thrown upon his face and figure, and is reflected from the front of the glass towards the spectators, who can thus see the reflected image, but not the hidden actor who produces it. For brevity's sake we will call this reflected image the phantom.

In order that the reflected light may come in a proper direction to the spectators, the glass is placed either upright or slightly leaning forward at the top, according to the height at which the seats of the spectators are placed. If the light is very strong on the hidden actor, and rather faint on the glass, the phantom appears with wonderful force and vividness. By means of a trap-door closing over the under-stage, the phantom may be made to disappear instantly; or by varying the intensity of the light, the phantom may seem to dissolve gradually.

Most of the subsequent patents relate to extensions of this method, with certain minor additions. Munro's patent (1863) is concerned chiefly with placing between the lamps and the hidden actor screens and media of various kinds, so as to let light fall on some parts, and leave others in darkness. In this way a phantom may be shown as if dismembered, head severed from the body, legs and arms separated, &c. By placing a movable mirror or silvered glass near the hidden actor, and shifting this while the action is going on the phantom may be made to go up and down and across the transparent glass. By the aid of two or more mirrors, the phantom may be magnified or diminished in size. By other arrangements, the visible actor may seem to enter a solid cube, or may seem to give a bottle or a letter to the phantom—effects due, in fact, to the superposition of a reflected image upon an object seen by transmitted light. Maurice's patent (1865), instead of causing a hidden actor to be reflected as a phantom, makes the visible actor himself become a sort of phantom before the eyes of the spectators. The phantom of a hidden object is supposed upon the real form of the actor, by nice adjustment; and then, if the light is dimmed which falls upon the actor, and the light brightened which falls upon the hidden object, the former will appear to fade away into invisibility; or the arrangements may be so managed as to make him seem to go through a solid wall, or be suspended in the air, or walking, or flying.

Reminders for Ghost Hunters

Those who go ghost hunting might be interested in the three scientific steps of what to do if you see a ghost.

1. *Keep calm.* Fiction and superstition have combined to make people regard ghosts as fearsome objects. In the main they are kind, gentle, and thoughtful beings, timorous and helpful.

2. *Be observant.* Note the appearance of the specter and what it does. Don't speak or attempt to touch it at first. Wait and see if it is going to make an approach to you. Note details of dress, features, height, movement, and position. See if material objects can be seen through it. Does it appear to walk through them?

3. If several people see it, seek their independent testimony.

Actors are perhaps collectively the most superstitious group of people in the world today; consequently there is a very strong belief in ghosts among them. This book is a collection of the best-known theater phantoms and many whose stories have never before appeared in print.

CHAPTER 2

North American Wraiths

The Ghost Called Anne

That a prison cell could become, within a few months, so horrifying that it had to be closed, never to house another convict, seems unlikely enough. That the succession of events which caused this were due to the ghost of an actress is even more unlikely. Yet no other alternative has ever been advanced to explain what happened to Cell Number 7 in the Fourth Precinct police station in New Orleans in 1872.

Early in the morning of November 10, 1872, Mary Taylor was cut down just in time by a jailer, who discovered that she had tried to hang herself by a makeshift rope made from strips of her cheap cotton dress. Dr. Paul Wessen, who had attended her, and Captain Doyle McKenna, a top-ranking detective, were summoned and between them the two men gradually extracted Mary Taylor's story from her.

She had awakened during the preceding night to see a luminous figure coming toward her. It was that of an elderly woman in a stained and crumpled dress and slippers. This figure had fixed her with such an intense stare that she had been unable to look away. The detective's casebook records that Mary Taylor said: "She compelled me to get up and tear my dress in strips and make a noose. I could not resist her terrible eyes. I fastened one end of the rope to the bars, put the noose around my neck—and then kicked my stool away."

As they listened to this and other details, Desk Sergeant Duggan and Captain McKenna realized that the girl had given an exact description of a drunken old woman—once an actress in New Orleans—named Anne Murphy, who had hanged herself in the same cell five months earlier. As a part of her theatrical life, Anne Murphy had been a stage hypnotist of remarkable talents. She had filled the music halls of New Orleans with the strangest feats anyone had seen. With her hypnotism she even induced people to steal for her.

The more recent history of that cell had been far more fantastic. Incredible as it now seems, since the day when the old actress had hanged herself, thirteen other prisoners had also committed suicide in it. In all that time the jailers had been trying to discover what was causing such a death list, and a suspicion had formed in their minds that the death of Anne Murphy had triggered off the situation. Now they appeared to have confirmation, but they were not satisfied. They decided to lay a trap for whatever nefarious agent was at work.

Searchers spent a long time tapping every brick in the cell, inspecting the bars, the grille, and every crack on the walls, floor, and ceiling. When they were satisfied that no human being could either make an entrance into the cell or cause anything to be passed through into it, they laid their trap.

The time came when they booked a Florida fisherman, a complete stranger to town, for a minor offense. After lengthy questioning, officers were satisfied that their captive had never even heard of Anne Murphy. Cell Number 7 was opened up and the slightly intoxicated fisherman gratefully sank down onto the bunk inside. Within a few minutes he was snoring loudly.

Outside in the corridor, Captain McKenna, Sergeant Duggan, and the jailer prepared to watch all night. Even though the three men were certain that nobody could enter without their knowledge, two patrolmen were also on watch outside the prison in a position immediately opposite the cell.

Every five minutes, one of the men in the corridor slid back the cell grille, and with the aid of a lantern, took a look at the sleeping prisoner. Soon after four o'clock, the fisherman's snoring stopped suddenly. Captain McKenna slid back the grille very slowly so as not to make the slightest sound. To his amazement, in the short time since the snores had ceased, the fisherman had fashioned a twisted cord from strips of his shirt, the other end of which was tied to one of the bars above.

McKenna bounded into the cell and slashed at the improvised rope with a knife. The other two men caught the prisoner as he buckled. Then they carried him along to McKenna's office, while all the time the prisoner kept shouting: "Keep her away from me! Keep her away from me!" After a few cups of black coffee the prisoner gave an account of the ghost, as Mary Taylor had done.

After that the cell was never used again for imprisonment—it became a storage room.

Copson's Traveling Theater

Around the late 1860's, Copson's Traveling Theater was a popular form of entertainment that visited the towns and hamlets of Minnesota, Wisconsin, and the Lake Superior side of Michigan. The name Copson was well known in the world of traveling entertainment, and this particular outfit was run by Ephraim T. Copson, Jr., whose grandfather had come to those parts from New York in 1847 with a traveling show.

To celebrate the incorporation of the city of Minneapolis in 1872, civic and neighborhood parties were held, and Copson's Traveling Theater set up on a site south of the city. For two days before the theater opened to the public, Mr. Copson sent the actors around the city delivering handbills to advertise the show. Three short plays were to be enacted every performance, with two vaudeville routines in between. The highlight of one of the between-play spots was Herman the Hypnotist, an act put on by a German actor called Herman Aikmann.

Copson's Theater comprised a stage on wheels, to which was fronted a huge tent for the audience, who sat on rough wooden benches. Flanking the paybox were booths of coconut shies and hooplas, and a stall selling sweetmeats and candy.

For this celebration show, a large crowd of folk came out from Minneapolis. A full ten minutes before the curtain rose, "House Full" notices went up, and every bench was filled with expectant crowds, cramming peanuts and popcorn into their mouths and sucking the sticky candy.

The first two plays and the fat lady on the donkey in the first vaudeville routine had met with loud applause and raucous amusement. A murmur went up from the crowd as the hypnotist was due to appear.

In the foul-smelling smoke of a firecracker, the hypnotist made a spectacular entrance. His tall figure, thin to the point of emaciation, his white made-up complexion and most of all his dark mascara-tinted eyelids and his large and sparking eyes compelled immediate attention. His garments, a very severe black suit and a black string tie, added a final Faustian touch.

With resignation and a kind of quiet contempt the hypnotist surveyed the audience. Then his sonorous voice reached to the far corners of the tent: "It is necessary for me to have a volunteer from among you." The accent was guttural and Germanic. "If some person would kindly step up . . ."

Everyone looked around and smirked, nudging his neighbor, but no one advanced to the worn stage.

The German hypnotist looked bored. "I can do no act unless someone comes up here with me." He lighted a cigarette and slouched against one of the flies. A little more kindly he said, "No one will get hurt, it is quite a harmless act, totally without danger."

He looked around expectantly, and presently a precocious-looking girl made her way up from the third row. The hypnotist bowed to her deliberately, sweeping the stage with his top hat, and helped her to a chair in the center of the stage.

"Relax," intoned the hypnotist. "Soon you will be asleep and you will do exactly what I tell you."

The girl leered cheekily and whispered something coarse to the hypnotist, who glared at her.

In a moment the hypnotist fixed the girl with his enormous painted eyes and the young woman tensed. Suddenly, out of the audience, someone threw a large ball of sticky taffy, which landed on the girl's head. She jerked slightly as if awaking from a dream, and the crowd yelled with delight.

The hypnotist went scarlet with rage; he faced the audience and shouted: "Who did that?"

The audience went unnaturally quiet.

At length the hypnotist stopped trembling with rage and returned to the girl, whom he dismissed with a wave of his hand. For a moment the hypnotist stalked around the stage, with hands behind his back, then he faced the audience once more.

"Perhaps the clown who threw the candy would care to assist me?"

Everyone in the audience now looked toward the figure of Archie Collins, who was sitting in the front row. The hypnotist caught the cue immediately and began to taunt the young man. Archie Collins was a daredevil—no real harm in him, just impudence. He sat and blushed as the audience began to shout: "Archie! Archie! Archie!" After a minute the young man could stand it no longer, and he raced up the rickety steps onto the stage.

All eyes were now back on the platform and folks began to murmur. Was it the footlights? The hypnotist's face looked more skeletal than ever.

The hypnotist motioned for young Collins to sit in the chair, and in under thirty seconds the lad was hypnotized and quite rigid. The hypnotist's voice droned on: "You are now asleep.

You will do anything I say. Remember, anything . . ."

Suddenly the hypnotist's tone changed to one of stifled excitement.

"Now, rise from the stage. Don't stand, rise as if you were a puppet."

The crowd drew a collective breath and murmured with fright, as Archie Collins hung in midair like a broken marionette.

"Rise, rise," went on the hypnotist as the boy floated above the band and the few front rows of the audience.

"Ha, ha, it's all a trick," someone shouted from the audience. "Cut him down, somebody." A ripple of laughter ensued. But most stared openmouthed as Collins floated nearer to the roof of the tent.

Abruptly the audience's attention left Archie as someone shouted: "Look at the hypnotist guy." And on stage the figure had transformed itself into a skeletal being, which slowly levitated itself a foot or so from the stage planking and then disappeared.

Thud! Thud! A sickening noise came from the roof of the tent as Archie's prone body encountered the canvas, and the body flipped over to show the boy's bruised face. Then the rotten canvas gave way and Archie Collin's body disappeared into the night air. Archie Collins was never seen again.

The boy's family reported him missing and the police visited Copson's Traveling Theater to investigate. Whoever the hypnotist was on the stage, they were assured, it was not Herman the Hypnotist as billed. Half an hour or so before the show started, the German had been taken ill with food poisoning, and was tended throughout the stage performance by his wife and Mr. Copson's personal assistant, Al Jones.

Herman Aikmann's son Ulrich had run to Copson's caravan and had told him of his father's sudden illness. After he had sent for the doctor, Copson had instructed the fat lady and her performing donkey to take the hypnotist's place. As she stood in the wings to go on, the fat lady had been pushed aside by a figure who resembled Herr Aikmann—but everybody now knew that it couldn't have been the German. Who was this strange figure who disappeared in front of the Minneapolis audience, and where did Archie Collins go? No one could offer an explanation, and the police file remains open.

Beatrice Lillie's Personal Poltergeist

Personal poltergeists are not unusual in theatrical circles. The late Sir Noel Coward certainly had one, which became a permanent tenant of his Chelsea studio in London. Although he never admitted seeing the ghost himself, several of his friends attested that they saw it. Coward always hinted that the spectral intruder inspired him to write his spook play *Blithe Spirit*. When Coward sold his London home and took up residence at Spithead Lodge, Warwick Parish, Bermuda, the ghost apparently went with him.

One of Noel Coward's best friends, Beatrice Lillie, the internationally celebrated comedienne, also had a personal poltergeist. The psychic experiences produced by this wraith were neither destructive nor unpleasant—only mischievous and embarrassing. Her poltergeist had apparently been following her around for years by the time she appeared at Palm Beach Playhouse in her show *An Evening with Beatrice Lillie*.

As Miss Lillie had a large dressing room, she allowed one of her troupe, Constance Carpenter, to keep one of her costumes there. Only three people had keys to the room: a maid, a dresser, and Beatrice Lillie herself. Before one particular performance Miss Carpenter discovered that she couldn't get into her costume—the skirt had been stitched all the way across the hem with coarse, yellowish cotton thread. She quickly ripped out the stitches and ran onto the stage just in time to answer her cue. After that she kept the costume in her own dressing room. No culprit was ever found.

During the second part of the show, Miss Lillie carried a small black fan. "One evening," she told theatrical columnist Danton Walker, "when I left my dressing room for the number just before the one when I used the fan, it was lying on my dressing-room table. My dresser locked the dressing-room door, as usual, and accompanied me to the stage. When we returned, the fan was nowhere to be seen! We searched *everywhere*, but couldn't find it, and I finally had to go on with another fan that I located in my wardrobe trunk.

"Two days later, the fan was back on my dressing-room table, in exactly the same place we had last seen it. There was no possible way for it, at the time, to have been put back without someone seeing the person doing it!"

In another of her numbers, Miss Lillie wore a Japanese wig, elaborately ornamented with decorative twigs. One evening she found that all the decorations had been removed from the wig and were laid in an orderly fashion on the dressing-room table. Again the door to the dressing room had been locked; none of the key holders could have tampered with the wig.

"But the time I *really* became annoyed," seethed Miss Lillie, "was when one of my rings disappeared—again from my dressing-room table. I looked everywhere for it—everywhere that I could think of—then, almost as if it were a compulsion from some unknown source, finally stood on a chair and looked to see what might be on a high shelf in the dressing room. And there on the shelf was the ring I had lost. That bloody poltergeist!"

Turner's Waxwork Theater

Madame Marie Tussaud (1761–1850), is probably the most famous of all exhibitors of waxworks. Born in Strasbourg, she had studied art with her uncle in Paris, and was appointed drawing mistress to the ill-fated family of Louis XVI of France. Coming to England in 1802, she settled in London, where her exhibition, first shown at the Lyceum in the Strand, became one of the most popular sights in the city.

During 1857, Richard Turner, a theatrical entrepreneur, visited the show and decided that an exhibition of waxworks was just what he wanted for a semipermanent show he desired to put on in Sacramento—then brimming with migrants who had streamed into California in the wake of James Wilson Marshall's discovery of gold at Sutter's mill, January 24, 1848.

As a nucleus for his collection, he bought from the Tussaud family a group of waxworks that had not proved popular with the London audiences. The group was that of six French actors who had gone to the guillotine during the Reign of Terror in Paris. Turner used these waxworks as the figures in a French Revolution guillotine scene, which he hoped would be gory enough to attract the hard-bitten miners.

Turner's Waxwork Theater made something of a splash in Sacramento and made more than a line or two in the local newspaper. Richard Turner was delighted that he had gone ahead with his enterprise. About a week after the show opened, however, a curious thing began to happen. Each morning when the janitor unlocked the room where the waxworks were kept, one of their number was never in the same position, and its wax head was always on the floor behind the figure. This went on for some weeks; although the room was securely locked and its exterior patrolled, the figure had always assumed a new position and the head was removed by the next morning.

Richard Turner and the janitor even spent a night in the room; they both fell asleep and woke up in the morning to find that the occurrence had taken place while they slept. They tried again, and this time they were more successful. Richard Turner left this record of what they saw: "It was remarkable; a little before 2:30 in the morning the figure of Monsieur Nicodème Léopold-Lépide began to move. First the arms and then the legs stirred. After a moment we saw the wax face take on a more flesh-and-blood image, and the brows frowned as if in anger and then we heard a voice."

The Waxwork Theater owner could not speak French, but he memorized what the voice had said. Later Richard Turner repeated what he and the janitor had heard to a French Canadian working in Sacramento.

"Is it not possible to get some peace at night," said the voice. "The people came to see us die, now they come to see our spirits encased in wax. Come here no more during the hours of darkness or you will regret it."

Somehow a journalist from a Sacramento newspaper heard of the strange encounter and asked if he could be allowed to stay in the room with the waxworks overnight to see for himself. Reluctantly Richard Turner agreed, and the young man was locked in the room. The janitor, however, remained outside the door all night. At exactly 2:31 the janitor was aroused by screams and hammerings coming from the room. He quickly unlocked the door, and the hysterical figure of the journalist slumped into his arms in a faint.

For his editor the journalist wrote up this account of what he had seen:

> The room where the waxworks are kept is square in shape with a vaulted roof. It is dimly lit with lamps on brackets all round the room. It was, by Mr. Turner's instructions, an eerie and uncomfortable chamber, inviting all who enter to talk in reverent whispers.
>
> The waxworks of the executed French men and women stand on individual podia, with neatly printed labels at their feet. There were five of them in all: Two aristocrats—a man and a woman—in their faded silks and lace (all taken from their bodies at death), a *curé* making a shop-window gesture with his Bible to a young lady-in-waiting, and a bland-looking man in a black suit and a frilled white *jabot*.
>
> I read the names. The man in the black suit was Nicodème Léopold-Lépide, about whom all the fuss was made. I knew nothing about him then, but have discovered since that he

was a tax-gatherer for a French *duc* and had won the hatred of milord's tenants by lining his pockets with their hard-earned *sous*.

As I sat in the gloom of the lamps, the dim wavering light fell on the rows of figures which were so uncannily like human beings that the silence and stillness of their forms made them seem even more unnatural and ghastly. I greatly missed the sound of breathing, the rustle of clothes and the perpetual sequence of noises one hears even when a deep silence has fallen over a vast crowd.

For an hour or two I sat facing the sinister figures boldly enough. They were, after all, only waxworks. Mr. Turner and old Ezra Potter, the janitor, must have been mistaken; this pile of smelly old wax couldn't move except with miner's blasting powder! This I kept telling myself.

Among the figures standing in their stiff unnatural poses, that of M. Léopold-Lépide, the effigy of the dreadful little taxman, did stand out with a queer prominence, perhaps because there was a lamp directly behind him.

Waxworks don't move. But every time I looked away from the taxman, when I looked back again he seemed to have struck a slightly different pose. I kept on looking and this time I saw something. The waxwork's arm did move. Slowly at first, then more rapidly to suddenly flick off its head! I stared, rather petrified, gripping the chair in which I sat. To my added horror where the waxwork head had been a ghostly visage now formed, with a cruel, rapacious leer.

It turned towards me and moved off its podium. I jumped up to face it, and the waxwork-ghost made towards me. What frightened me the most was the way I could see through its head!

Backing to the door I tapped on it to get the janitor to see the phenomena. There was no answer. I banged hard this time, as the waxwork-ghost moved closer. I turned and started to bang my fists on the door. I screamed too as I felt the horrid wax hands close round my neck. I screamed again and can't remember any more, only the welcoming face of Ezra Potter.

I would swear by all that is holy that this that I have written is true.

Next morning the head of the waxwork of M. Léopold-Lépide was found on the floor next to the other figures. Strangely, the body was over by the door in a heap. Yet the fingers of the waxwork were flat and displaced—as if the wax had been softened and gone out of shape. Could this have been done when they pressed against the journalist's neck?

The waxwork was melted down and replaced by another figure in the scene, and thereafter there were no further strange movements. The Turner Waxwork Theater was to operate until 1885, when it was supplanted by live theater in Sacramento. The journalist's story never appeared in print in the local press, and for some reason the editor decided to spike the story. The tale only came to light in the 1930's on the death of the journalist.

Metropolitan Opera House Ghost

James Reynolds, artist and designer who won fame for his sets of the *Greenwich Village Follies*, always averred that the Metropolitan Opera House, New York, which was first built on Thirty-ninth Street in 1883, was haunted. Reynolds often recounted the story of a woman friend who attended a matinee alone about 1955. Apparently the woman had not intended going to the opera alone, but at the last minute the friend she was to go with canceled the date. So the woman sold the extra ticket back to the Met box office.

As she settled herself in the seat, Reynolds' friend became more and more annoyed by the person who had turned up to occupy the seat where her friend was to have sat. Her neighbor was now a thickset, busty woman, dressed in a silk suit that rustled every time she moved. The person also crackled her program noisily, on purpose it seemed, and whenever the leading soprano in the opera sang an aria, she would nudge Reynolds' friend on the arm and hiss, "Flat, flat, *flat!*"

Shushing this woman seemed of no use, so the friend of James Reynolds went to complain to the manager. One of the ushers went down the aisle to investigate, but on his return reported to the manager that the seat in question was empty and had been so since the beginning of the performance, according to the people around.

Once again the ghost of Mme. Frances Alda had appeared, it seemed—as she had several times before. As the wife of director Giulio Gatti-Casazza, she had been well known for her loud comments on the performances of her rivals. Time and again in life she had sat in the stalls and made rude remarks about the acting and singing of the artists—her favorite comment being "Flat, flat, *flat!*" Even in death she returned to deride.

Strange to report, when Reynolds' friend got home, she found that her arm was black and blue from the nudging.

The Unlucky Theater

For a score or so of years, there stood in New York's Broadway a theater called the New Theater. It was regarded as unlucky by those in the theatrical profession because for a very long time no play produced there had been a success. Many thought that it had a forbidding supernatural aura about it that inhibited prosperity.

An old actor called Charles O'Farrell became interested in the occult aspects of the theater and as a psychic person himself asked the then owner of the theater if he could spend a night in the theater to investigate any preternatural qualities it might have. The owner raised no objection to O'Farrell's vigil, provided that he did not supply any comment to the newspapers. This was agreed, and it was arranged that O'Farrell should go the stage door an hour after curtainfall on a Monday night.

O'Farrell arrived in time and was let in at the stage door by the night watchman, whose place O'Farrell had agreed to take without pay. After the watchman had conducted O'Farrell around the theater and showed him how to cope in case of fire, the old actor was left alone.

The theater seemed uncomfortably lonely, and after the watchman had gone, there was an eerie and depressing stillness about, unbroken except by creakings in the woodwork. O'Farrell—who had spent some fifty years acting—never realized that a theater could be so quiet. For half an hour or so he wandered up and down staircases and along the corridors, lamp in hand, peering into boxes, side rooms, and cupboards. Then he went backstage. Thick dust lay on the piles of ropes, pieces of torn scenery, and grubby costumes, and there were signs of long neglect everywhere.

For a while O'Farrell thumbed through an album of faded theater bills he had found, and as he put the volume back on a ledge, he heard a movement in the stage manager's room. He cautiously pushed the door of the room open and saw a man, with a folio in his hand, pacing up and down as if he were learning lines. On hearing the door open, the man stopped and stared at O'Farrell, a guilty, startled look in his eyes.

The watchman had told O'Farrell that there was no one in the theater, so what was the man doing there? There was something very odd about him. He wore clothes in fashion some twenty years before and somehow didn't look quite real. O'Farrell noticed too that the man's shirt front was stained with what looked like blood—probably propman's dye, he thought.

"What are you doing? Who are you?" asked O'Farrell, holding his lamp up to get a better look at the man. As he stepped forward, however, the man inexplicably vanished. For a moment the old Irish actor was stunned, but continued, a little shakily, his rambling around the musty old theater.

Around one o'clock in the morning, O'Farrell sat himself in

the pit and ate his sandwiches and drank hot coffee. Over the top of his cup as he drained it, he saw a dark-haired woman climb up onto the stage, look around the house, and disappear through the curtain. "Hey!" shouted the actor, clambering up onto the stage after her. But she too had vanished.

Maybe an hour or more passed, and O'Farrell was getting bored—not tired, just bored. He settled himself in the front row of the stalls and looked around him at the seedy decor. Although it was a summer evening, the theater felt cold, and the actor distinctly felt "that feeling" coming on.

Charles O'Farrell was a good Roman Catholic and didn't have anything to do with spiritualism. In spite of his beliefs, however, from childhood he had had the talents of a spiritualistic medium; fight it how he might, he involuntarily had associations with spirits of the dead. As he sat there in the dark, he experienced the familiar bodily numbness he knew preceded all his manifestations.

The theater began to take on a fresh, new, clean look, and the auditorium was bathed in golden light from the sparkling chandeliers above. Around him people began to take form, all in costumes of a bygone era. In minutes the dress circle, the balcony, pit, boxes, and gallery were no longer empty. Yet the faces of these people were corpse-like in their pallor.

Looking around him, O'Farrell saw a woman seated alone in one of the boxes. It was the woman he had seen a few minutes before. She was now dressed in a beautiful plum-colored dress and no longer wore the dark-blue cloak she'd had on when he saw her first. The woman was leaning forward, staring fixedly at the stage.

This was a most remarkable materialization, the best O'Farrell had ever experienced, affecting all the senses but one—smell. Charles O'Farrell distinctly heard the sound of the orchestra playing. At length the curtain rose, and for five minutes or so a play unfolded. Yes, there on stage was the man O'Farrell had seen in the stage manager's room. The man was seated at a desk reading, when a young man burst in from the right and shot the seated actor. The curtain descended for the end of scene one, and the whole set of revenants dematerialized. Not before O'Farrell, however, saw the lady in the box jump to her feet applauding enthusiastically.

Charles O'Farrell went back to the watchman's booth and had no further occult adventures that night.

The owner of the theater was interested in O'Farrell's story, and told the old Irish actor of a tragedy that had occurred at a theater on the same site some three decades before. A play *The Boss* was then on at the theater and starred John Nares and David P. Teales. Nares, it appears, was very much in love with Teales's wife Laura, who led the young man on and repeatedly swore that she hated her husband, who was, she said, cruel to her.

In this play John Nares had to rush onstage and pretend to shoot "the boss," David Teales. In reality live bullets were fired, and unbeknown to the audience, Teales was killed instantly. It was always subsequently thought that Laura Teales bribed the property man to switch the blanks for live bullets. Whether or not Nares was a party to this is not known. After the "accident" John Nares and Laura Teales vanished.

"Since that time," the owner explained to Charles O'Farrell in his office the next morning when the actor recounted his night's adventures, "the theater has been deemed haunted."

It is interesting to note that Charles O'Farrell knew nothing of the Nares–Teales story before he kept vigil.

The New Theater is long departed from the Broadway scene and is long forgotten; the site was subsequently sold.

Did Chinese Spirits Reclaim a Theater?

Under the dateline "Vancouver, December 13, 1947," Ted Greenslade made this report to the paper *Saturday Night*:

Oxen plowed through the mud on Granville Street, the Klondike Gold Rush was yet to be heard of, and cutting off the pig-tails of Chinese was a popular sport with young bloods, when the Sing Kew Society took over a building on Carrall Street and made it into Vancouver's first Chinese theatre.

Last week this landmark burned, and in the flames died not only four Chinese but the ghosts of a lot of the yesterdays of men who played a part in the pioneering of Canada. . . .

Of late years the building had been partitioned off to make sleeping cubicles and workshops, and there are those among the Chinese who believe some ghostly prompting may have started the fire.

To the ancient Chinese, society goes down the scale from the artist and teacher, to the artisan, to the farmer, and then to the soldier. "Perhaps," claim the ancients, "the spirits who haunted the theatre know that the ancient drama is dying. They have seen the house lose face. Old Chinese know it is preferable that one dies. The fire will make the spirits of the past truly dead."

1938617

The Spook Who Promoted a Play

Ghosts are not always helpful to actors and actresses. Kim Novak, for instance, when she was filming *Moll Flanders*, was terrified by the venerable ghost of the Lady in White, who has shared the Norman castle home of successive Viscounts Massereine and Ferrard at Chilham, Kent, England, since the Middle Ages.

Miss Novak is probably the first American postwar victim of the ghostly lady, who has the disconcerting habit of wafting herself at midnight through the ancient slabs of the dungeons at Chilham Castle. Kim Novak caught sight of the ghost on the dungeon stairs and got such a fright that she fell down the steps and was injured. This haunting stems from the time when an unknown lady was bricked up in one of the walls by the order of Lord Bartholomew de Badlesmere (who was later beheaded for treason by King Edward I).

Impresario Guthrie McClintic, however, had nothing but good to say about ghosts. His particular phantom advised him to support the play *The Barretts of Wimpole Street* after it had been turned down by some twenty-eight producers. McClintic described the psychic story in his memoirs.

Another great theater man, David Belasco, saw a ghost and wrote a play.

David Belasco (1853–1931) was to become one of America's most famous dramatists. Born in San Francisco, the son of Humphrey Abraham Belasco, an English Jew, David Belasco first appeared at the Metropolitan Theater at San Francisco and went on to be stage manager of the Madison Square Theater in New York. He is best remembered for his plays *Hearts of Oak* (1880), *La Belle Russe* (1882), *May Blossom* (1884), *Valerie* (1886), and *The Girl of the Golden West* (1905). He was later owner and manager of the Belasco Theater in New York.

In the 1920's the psychic researcher Ida Clyde Clarke made a study of a curious ghost story concerning Belasco, of which this is her full report:

On a snowy November evening in 1903, David Belasco arrived at his Newport home exhausted in mind and body. He was in the midst of rehearsing *Zara*, a play whose ownership was in dispute. In his comfortable library, with his adored young daughter Augusta sitting on the arm of his chair, he relaxed and his mood grew soft and reminiscent. The night before, Augusta had seen a rehearsal of *Zara*, and he asked her opinion of it, for he always said she was his best critic.

Augusta didn't like the play, and she told him so. "Father," she said, "I wish you'd do a story of the supernatural sometime. It is a subject in which everybody is interested."

Her father smiled at her and shook his head. "Not after the River of Souls in *The Darling of the Gods*!" he said, reminding her of the trouble he had had with special effects in a previous production.

They laughed together, but as he kissed her good night she

turned serious once more. "Promise me you *will* do a play dealing with the supernatural."

"You write the play and I will produce it," he answered.

Feeling rested and relaxed, he soon fell into a deep sleep. Shortly after midnight he awoke with a start. Feeling a presence in the room, he looked up and saw his mother standing beside his bed, gazing down upon him. He knew that she was in San Francisco, yet there she was standing close to him.

He made an effort to speak, to rise, but he could not move nor utter a sound.

Then his mother, whom he had always loved tenderly, smiled and said, "Davy, Davy, Davy!"

There was an infinite tenderness in her eyes, and she leaned down and kissed him. "Do not grieve for me. All is well and I am happy." Then she moved toward the door and vanished.

Almost immediately he again fell into a restful sleep. Next morning he told his experience at the breakfast table, but the family laughed and told him it was only a dream.

"Your mother is well and in San Francisco," his wife said. "Had she been ill, we would have heard."

As he kissed Augusta good-bye that morning, he whispered, "I know that my dear mother is dead, Augusta, I *know* it."

When he reached his office, he found a telegram stating that his mother had died at the precise hour he had seen her standing beside his bed. Later he learned that just before she died, she spoke of him and called his name—"Davy, Davy, Davy!"

That night, Augusta went to her father's room to try once more to say something that would comfort him. As she sat beside him, he took her hand and said:

"My little guardian, now we will write a great play. It will deal with the actual return of the dead—for the dead do return. My mother has convinced me by coming back to me at the moment of her death."

That experience resulted in one of Belasco's most famous plays, *The Return of Peter Grimm*. When the play was first produced in Boston, October 18, 1911, the printed program contained a statement from David Belasco to the effect that he had been inspired to write and produce the play by his mother's appearance to him at the time of her death.

Many believe that Belasco haunts his own theater. In life the playwright had been something of a poseur; he decorated his living quarters like a monastery and wore a monk's habit. Actors from time to time, it seems, have seen him sitting in his favorite stage box—a dim shade behind the plush curtains —his features clearly visible and his monk's cowl pushed down.

Folk say too that the elevator of the Belasco Theater can be heard whirring up and down of its own accord after eleven o'clock at night. Belasco's ghost on its way to the actor's former rooms at the top of the theater perhaps? At night, too, when the theater is empty and in darkness, laughter can be heard, footsteps and singing and doors opening and shutting with a bang. But most unnerving of all, the front curtain mysteriously raises, hovers, and lowers itself.

CHAPTER 3

An American President
Walks the Boards

Haunted theaters in America are few and far between, probably because most don't have much antiquity. One, however, is the center of a classic American ghost story.

Ford's Theater, in Washington, is little more than a hundred years old. Today it is best known for being the location of Abraham Lincoln's assassination on April 14, 1865, by an unsuccessful actor from a famous theatrical family, John Wilkes Booth. The story has been often told, but basically it can be said that the assassin broke into the theater's presidential box and emptied his Derringer pistol into Lincoln's head. Booth made his escape by leaping over the rim of the box and onto the stage. Running diagonally across the stage, the fanatical actor fled into the street. He was shot to death in the subsequent pursuit on April 26, in a burning barn on a farm near Port Royal, Virginia.

Time and the delving of journalists and occult researchers have produced a haunting theory concerning Ford's Theater. To understand it, however, a look into Abraham Lincoln's own attitude toward ghosts is worthwhile.

Perhaps President Abraham Lincoln (1809–65) is the best-known spiritualist ever to occupy the White House. A short while after he became the sixteenth President of the United States, the *Cleveland Plain Dealer* published a feature story stating that Lincoln believed in ghosts and was keenly interested in psychic studies. The article was shown to Lincoln and he commented: "This article does not begin to tell the wonderful things I have witnessed. Half of it has not been told."

It is not surprising, therefore, that Lincoln's assassination has a psychic aura about it. The story of President Lincoln's own "trance dream" of his assassination is well known. Gideon Welles, one of the members of Lincoln's Cabinet, left this recollection of what the President had himself said: "President Lincoln said that his dream was focused on water and that he was sailing in a singular, but indescribable vessel; in it he seemed to float towards a shore he knew was ultimate death; this dream had occurred to him before the battles of Bull Run, Antietam, Gettysburg, Stone River, Vicksburg, Wilmington and so on. This was the scenario too for a trance dream of his own death."

In his papers the late Lord Halifax left this account of Lincoln's premonitory dream:

> Several years ago, Mr. Charles Dickens, as we know, went on a tour of America. Among other places he visited Washington, where he called upon his friend, the late Mr. Charles Sumner, the well-known senator who was present at Lincoln's death. After talking of various matters, Mr. Sumner said to Dickens: "I hope that you have seen everybody and everything that you wanted to see, that there is no wish unfulfilled."
>
> "Well," replied Dickens, "there is one person whose acquaintance I greatly wish to make, and that is Mr. Stanton."
>
> "Oh, that is very easily managed," Sumner assured him. "Mr. Stanton is a great friend of mine. Come and meet him here."
>
> So it was arranged, and much conversation passed. Towards midnight, before the three men separated, Stanton turned to Sumner and said: "I should like to tell Mr. Dickens that story about the President."
>
> "Well," said Sumner, "the time is very suitable."
>
> Stanton proceeded as follows:

"During the war, as you know, I was in charge of all the troops in [the District of] Columbia, and as you may imagine, I had my hands pretty full. One day there was a council ordered for two o'clock but I was pressed with business and could not get there till twenty minutes past. When I entered, most of my colleagues were looking rather grave, but I thought nothing of that, nor of the words that fell from the President as I entered: 'But gentlemen, this is not business; here is Mr. Stanton.' Business proceeded and various matters were discussed and settled. When the Council broke up, I walked away arm in arm with the Attorney General, saying to him as we left: 'Well, we have really done some work today. The President applied himself to business, instead of flitting about from one chair to another, talking to this and that man.' 'Ah,' said the Attorney General, 'but you were not here at the beginning; you do not know what passed.' 'What did pass?' I asked. 'When we entered the Council Chamber today,' resumed the Attorney General, 'we found the President seated at the top of the table with his face buried between his hands. Presently he raised it, and we saw that he looked grave and worn. He said, 'Gentlemen, before long you will have important news.' We all enquired, 'What, sir, have you had bad news? Is it anything serious?' He replied, 'I have heard nothing; I have had no news; but you will hear tomorrow.' We again pressed him to tell us what had happened, and at last he said, 'I have had a dream; I have dreamt that dream three times—once before the battle of Bull Run, once on another occasion, and again last night. I am in a boat, alone—on a boundless ocean. I have no oars—no rudder—I am helpless. I drift! I drift! I drift!' "

"Five hours afterwards the President was assassinated."

Ford's Theater fell into disuse a few years after Lincoln's assassination; it remained abandoned for a century. In 1968, however, the Ford's Theater Society restored it as a working theater, and as a museum of theatrical relics and of "assassination souvenirs." Since its opening many have experienced the local "presence." In the main the hauntings are in the form of sound and temperature changes—the sound of footsteps and the chilling of the atmosphere before certain enactments take place, like curtains raising and lowering of their own accord. One stagehand, it appears, was so unnerved by the laughter of spook voices that he fled while changing to go home, finding himself minutes later in the street in his underpants.

There is a uniqueness about the spook or spooks at Ford's Theater, for here is to be found the "occult line." That "line" is the route Booth took making his escape. Actors and actresses standing on, or near, the route of the assassin's flight have often been afflicted in unusual and disturbing ways—nausea, nervousness to the point of shuddering, and loss of memory. Some even forget where they are to an extent never before experienced in their careers. Both Hal Holbrook ("Mark Twain") and Jack Aronson ("Herman Melville") have testified to the "power of going near the occult line."

The Spanish actor Mandogel de Mandala (1872–1928) was once taken to the then-derelict theater by a friend, to view the scene of Lincoln's assassination. During the visit the friend begged to be excused and for a while Mandala was left alone in the auditorium. Sitting himself in one of the dusty seats, the actor looked toward the fateful box—ah! there was his friend again! No, it couldn't be, the friend could not have aged that much in a few minutes, nor have changed into a frock coat. Of course, too, the friend was clean shaven.

Mandala watched the figure sit down in the box and slump forward—a few seconds later he heard a voice give a hoarse laugh and say (Mandala could speak no English) what sounded like "Ahdreft."

In a moment Mandala's friend returned and the actor explained what he had seen. "It couldn't have been me," the friend said in Spanish. "I was at the other side of the theater."

Was "Ahdreft" in fact "I drift"—maybe the wraith of Abraham Lincoln making one of its appearances?

Ford's Theater certainly has its fair share of occultism. Just after the assassination, Matthew Brady took a photograph of the empty theater and the negative revealed a transparent figure standing inside the Presidential box. Did Brady freeze for all time the ghost of Lincoln? Or maybe even Booth?

CHAPTER 4

Harry Houdini's Encounters

Harry Houdini (1874–1926), son of a Hungarian rabbi, was born Ehrich Weiss in Appleton, Wisconsin. He called himself Houdini after the French magician Jean Robert-Houdin. Houdini first attracted special notice as a conjuror by his handcuff escapes, which he claimed to have perfected when he was apprenticed to a locksmith; many times he had freed jammed handcuffs as a part of his daily work. Houdini's other escapes, on which his fame chiefly rested, were from prisons (baffling in every case the authorities who had challenged him), mailbags, straitjackets (sometimes while suspended upside down), trunks, and glass boxes. Several of the escapes were carried out under water. Even though many of his tricks depended upon specially prepared apparatus, the basis of Houdini's success in America, Britain, Europe, and Russia was a dexterity and boldness unmatched by his fellow illusionists.

The American magician developed a keen interest in the occult, and devoted a large amount of his time to uncovering the tricks of fraudulent spiritualistic mediums, who for two dollars a time entertained at house parties, theaters, and séance rooms.

A Brother's Call

Although a professional skeptic—he insisted that he could duplicate all *known* phenomena of supernatural modern designation by natural methods—Houdini "wanted to believe that ghosts exist" and collected a large amount of data on psychic phenomena. On his death a number of papers were found which contained notes on haunted theaters and strange ghostly events connected with the theatrical profession. One such was quoted by psychic investigator Ida Clyde Clarke:

Harry Kellar was one of the most noted magicians of his time, and was a great friend of Houdini's. By virtue of his remarkable skill he was known to the fraternity of magicians as "Dean Kellar." He not only performed amazing feats himself, but he discovered and trained for the American theatrical circuit some of the best magicians of the day.

Among his protégés were two brothers, Ling Look and Yamadeva, and with these expert performers he toured the world, including many of the theatres in which Houdini himself performed. . . .

When Harry Kellar and his performers arrived in China, Ling Look and Yamadeva were very happy. Though they had not a drop of Chinese blood in their veins—being Hungarian born—they always appeared in Chinese costume, and all of their young lives they had wanted to see China.

They were showing in Shanghai, and after the evening performance they would wander about the city in search of adventure. Yamadeva was very fond of bowling, and [got into an exciting match one night with a sea captain]. . . . Yamadeva seized one of the largest balls and drove it down the alley with all his might, but no sooner had he delivered the ball than he grasped his side and moaned in pain. The next instant he had crumpled to the floor.

Half an hour later, in a hospital, they told Ling Look that Yamadeva was dead, that he had ruptured an artery in that last fierce drive of the ball.

Harry Kellar and his troupe were leaving early next morning for their next engagement in Hong Kong. Kellar did what he could to console Ling Look, and he set about making plans for the burial.

But the boy said: "I cannot leave Yamadeva in Shanghai. . . . If he stays, I stay."

And they could not move him from his decision.

To pacify the heartbroken boy, and in the hope that he would become reconciled to his loss after a few days, Kellar decided to take Yamadeva's body to Hong Kong. But the Chinese had their own ideas about the bodies of the dead and the captain of the steamer *Khiva*, upon which they had engaged passage, was not disposed to co-operate in the plan. However, he was finally persuaded—not by American eloquence, but by American money—to take the corpse of Yamadeva aboard.

All day on the boat Ling Look was very sad. He would not talk, but stood at the rail and stared into the river.

At midnight he rushed into Kellar's cabin, greatly excited.

"My brother is not dead!" he cried. "He is alive. He has whistled to me several times—the whistle no one knows —we always used it as a signal in our act—I tell you Yamadeva is alive! Open the coffin, quick!"

According to Houdini's story, which was told to him many times by Harry Kellar: "The whistle was several times repeated and was heard by all on board."

Passengers and crew gathered around the weeping Ling Look. Now and then he would suddenly become very quiet and raise his finger. A moment later they would hear the low, peculiar whistle.

At first the Captain refused to open the coffin, but when he heard the whistle he consented to investigate.

It was midnight. The boat was moving swiftly and steadily. In great solemnity the passengers and crew gathered round while the lid of the coffin was removed.

Ling Look's face was very pale and very calm. Some one held a light above the coffin, and he leaned over the still body and looked into the face of Yamadeva.

There was no sign of life.

When Ling Look raised his head he was pitiful to see.

"I will never leave Hong Kong alive," he said. "My

brother has called me to join him. I have always obeyed that call."

The day after their arrival in Hong Kong Ling Look was taken seriously ill, and was carried to the hospital. He underwent an operation and died under the knife.

The two brothers were buried in Happy Valley, Hong Kong.

The Ghost That Committed Murder

While playing in Washington, D.C., Houdini did some research into the stories of the city's two famous ghosts: the angry shade of Pierre L'Enfant, the city's designer, who is said to walk the basement of the Capitol, and that of President Lincoln at the White House. During his talks with people, he came across a woman called Amy Irving who made her name as an actress in a little repertory company that used to be on E Street N.W.

Amy Irving had married twice: Harry Colona, who had died after the birth of their second child, and Arthur Gilman, a fellow actor. Gilman had little talent as an actor, and less talent to look for other work. He was one of those actors who only find work at New Year or Halloween. For over twenty years, Gilman was a character actor in the small theater circuits of the West Coast, working in shows that needed a ghost, a murderer, an undertaker, or a sinister old uncle. It wasn't that he was outright ugly, it was just that he had an air of death about him—to such an extent that no one liked working with him. Between seasons he was lucky if he got a week's engagement with a concert party.

When Houdini met Amy Irving, Gilman had been dead for some years—killed in 1911, it was said, by a ghost.

One particular Christmas, Gilman had been hired, with a group of other entertainers, to act and play at a party held by a government official in one of the larger houses in Georgetown. For a fee equal to a month's salary on the boards,

Gilman acted at the party as a stooge for a conjuror, danced with spinster guests, and took part in a bloodcurdling dramatic tale.

Entertainers and guests mingled at suppertime and sat around a huge log fire. Then came the moment when the door of the party room crashed open.

Startled rather than frightened, all eyes turned to the door.

There in the light of the flickering fire stood a tall man in a shimmering white suit, black opera mask, and cloak. What could be seen of the flesh of the face was of corpselike hue.

One or two of the girls squealed with terror. But for the most part the guests guffawed with laughter.

The white-clad man waved his arms up and down several times, as if he were doing some trick, and advanced with long, gliding paces into the room. From his mouth he uttered a groaning noise that sent shivers down most spines.

Who could he be? The host had a quick look around at his guests to see if one was missing. No, they were all there. What about the entertainers? He had employed five, and five were there eating their supper. No doubt the stranger was a gate crasher. The host nodded to Arthur Gilman to find out who the stranger was.

Gilman put down his plate and walked over to the figure. He was seen to say something, and suddenly he fell to the ground as if he had been poleaxed. Someone screamed and to the amazement of all those present, the figure vanished, leaving only a pile of clothes. Gilman was dead. His skull had been fractured by a heavy blow.

Houdini was fascinated by the story. It seemed to him a case of escape-illusion par excellence. How had the stranger done it? He had to find out.

The illusionist traced the name of the government official at whose house the party had taken place. The official, however, had died a year after the party and the house had been sold. The present owners knew nothing about the story. Houdini researched more and found some of the people who had been at the party. Most could not help with his inquiries, but one lady, Gladys Pedler, was able to tell him of a strange conclusion to the affair.

The police had been called in but had been unable to make any arrest. Each guest had a perfect alibi—each other. Miss Pedler, however, knew the neighborhood well and could remember the previous owner of the house. Harry grew excited when he heard the name of the owner—George Hayman, one of America's most dexterous amateur illusionists. He had died in the house in 1907.

Before he died, it was common knowledge that Hayman had "gone funny." He became a recluse and was violent to anyone who came near him. Ultimately he committed suicide by hanging himself from the staircase.

"It was a shock to me, I can tell you," said Miss Pedler. "I knew Georgie Hayman in the old days. He always wore a white shiny suit and a mask when he went to entertain at church socials and the like. That was George Hayman all right, standing there in the doorway. I went hot and cold all down my spine when I saw him. The pile of clothes left after he disappeared were certainly his—his sister later identified them. But on that night George had been dead some four years."

Puzzle it out how he might, Houdini could not come to a logical answer. There were no trapdoors in either floor or ceiling and no hidden lights or screens to cause illusion—the Arthur Gilman case was undoubtedly supernatural.

The Shuffling Footsteps

This was not the only brush with the unknown Houdini had. One occurred during his last trip to Boston. The theater where he gave his performance was haunted, or so members of the staff told him.

When the theater was being built, a workman mysteriously disappeared without collecting his wages. His lunchbox, cap, and coat were found hanging on a hook near that part of the building that became the stage. The workman seems to have disappeared one lunch break without trace, and there was speculation that something sinister had happened to him that never came to light.

The ghostly happenings at the Boston Theater—as it was once called—were centered on shuffling footsteps heard from the direction of the empty stage late at night by several members of the staff, including the theater manager. The footsteps, Houdini was told, were so frequent in their occurrence that people took little notice of them.

Houdini reported the manager as saying at the time: "There is simply no normal explanation for the noises. I have heard them on dozens of occasions, while working late. I've had floorboards ripped up, plumbing checked, but nothing of a mechanical fault of nature has been discovered. To me, the noises sound as though someone is shuffling about across the stage. The first time I heard it I was alone in the theater and thought it was a burglar. I got the cops in, but they found no one. Every time the noises occur, the windows and doors have been tightly shut."

Has Harry Houdini Himself Returned

On October 31, 1926, Harry Houdini died in the arms of his wife, and soon after speculation was rife that the great illusionist would attempt to cheat death and appear himself in ghost form. Did Houdini make a final escape from the realm we call death? Did he successfully communicate with his wife, using the spiritualistic medium Arthur Ford and a secret code? Most people are as skeptical as Houdini would have been himself.

Mrs. Beatrice Houdini at first most definitely attested that a message had come through from her dead husband. She signed a statement to that effect and confirmed it in a letter to gossip columnist Walter Winchell of January 19, 1929. Later she began to wonder if the messages actually were from Houdini, and she doubted right up to her death in 1934. Some, however, still think that Houdini's ghost is active.

Take, for instance, the Palace Theater story.

On a number of occasions the ghost of a tightrope walker has been seen at the Palace Theater in New York. Some have even seen his spectral death fall and heard his cry of fear as he plummets to the ground. Peter Grey took some photographs of the place where the ghost was seen and to his surprise the negative showed a "psychic extra"—the head and shoulders of a man later identified as Harry Houdini.

The puzzle is that the ghost at the Palace only dates from the 1950's, a quarter of a century after Houdini's death. In fact, the ghost is thought to be of vaudeville acrobat Louis Borsalino, who was mortally injured here in the 1950's. Perhaps Houdini's ghost is not fussy as to whose psychic act he gets in on.

Actor Richard Huggett recorded a story about Jay Fox, the director and choreographer who has also had contact with the shade of Houdini.

It seems that Fox was preparing to mount a musical of the life of Harry Houdini, a project that was jinxed from the start by numerous problems: investors reneged; actors left the cast at the last minute; the script was the wrong length; and technical difficulties dogged the production. Eventually the cast got into rehearsal at a small theater somewhere in the country.

One day—when depression caused by setbacks was at its highest—someone suggested that they consult the Fates, using a Ouija board. The company did so, any suggestion from "the other world" being deemed welcome, and this message was received: "I'll send a sign." Gloom was lifted instantly at the thought of Houdini's spirit communicating directly.

To advertise the show, it was decided to decorate the outside of the theater with strips of tinfoil. Huggett says that a gusty breeze came along almost from nowhere on that sunny day, and to the company's astonishment the wafting lengths of tinfoil formed themselves into a large *H*. Harry Houdini, it was supposed, was trying to reassure them that all would be well. The opening performance of the musical took place at Stephanie Barber's house, Wheatleigh. Eyewitnesses say that during the performance a trunk used for Houdini's escape suddenly acquired on its front a large *H*. It certainly had not been there before, and nobody had any idea who had painted it. The work of Houdini's ghost, it was said.

What was Harry Houdini's favorite theatrical ghost story?

Those who cleared out Houdini's papers on his death thought they knew. Penciled notes and newspaper cuttings were found to reveal a curious ghost-murder story that Houdini was piecing together when he died. All the evidence was put together to form the following tale of mystery.

Grandmother's Legacy

In bygone days a favorite theater with Los Angeles playgoers was the Primrose, located near Hill Street. Here the Primrose Theater Company put on plays for over twenty years.

The company had been started by Arnold Gibson, grandfather of its most famous owner, Rosemary Primrose Adelaide Gibson Myers, whose family had fought in the Mexican War. As Miss Gibson, Rosemary Myers had cut a dash in vaudeville in New York and Washington. Around 1897, just about the time oil was struck in California and industry began to be developed, she took over the Los Angeles theater from her father.

Now long demolished, the Primrose Theater did not have an impressive frontage; in fact, it looked more like a large candy shop than a theater. At the top of the stairs leading to the small auditorium, theatergoers would often stop and admire an old clock. The case for the clock had been made to order for the Gibson family by Prudent Mallard, in his Royal Street shop in New Orleans; the clock was of lemonwood and rosewood and stood on a fine pedestal.

The old timepiece was Rosemary Myers' pride and joy. She wound it carefully every day. The sound of its penetrating, ratchety, creaking spring was a sign to other people in the theater that the old lady was going to bed, just as its loud morning strike announced to the staff that she was about to come down from her flat above the theater.

Mrs. Myers always told her granddaughter, Shirlee-Ann, that the clock would be hers one day. Mrs. Myers had brought Shirlee-Ann up herself, after the death of the girl's father and mother in an accident at sea. Shirlee-Ann was a precocious, arrogant, and conceited child, but Mrs. Myers saw in her some talent for the stage and expected to bequeath her the Primrose. In particular, she wished to see her granddaughter as fond of the old clock as she was herself.

But Shirlee-Ann was not interested in acting and loathed the old clock. When Mrs. Myers sent her to New York to learn theater management, she neglected her training in favor of devoting herself to a young actor who had caught her fancy. His name was Leonard Banks. He refused to marry her, but she went to live with him in his apartment nevertheless. When her grandmother learned of this arrangement, she cut Shirlee-Ann out of her will and left the theater and its contents to her nephew instead.

Some six months later, Rosemary Myers fell ill with a heart complaint and had a change of heart. Shirlee-Ann was sent for. "Have you married that horrid man?" Mrs. Myers asked her granddaughter, and when the girl answered—quite truthfully—no, the old lady was pleased. "I hope you are remembering to wind the clock?"

"Oh, yes, Grandmother."

Shirlee-Ann, in fact, confronted the clock every day. As she opened the door of the clock and looked at the arrangement of pulleys, weights, and ropes, it reminded her of a stomach. The clock had a face, head, and hands; somehow it was almost human, with its pendular heartbeat. Because she hated it, the knowledge that she had power over the mechanism gave Shirlee-Ann a thrill. She had only to stop winding it, and the clock would die.

That night Shirlee-Ann overheard Mrs. Myers giving her servant instructions to go for her attorney, "because I wish to alter my will."

Next day, after the midday meal, the family lawyer came and went, and an hour later a messenger arrived with a sealed envelope for Mrs. Myers. Shirlee-Ann looked at it. It was the very shape and size of a new will. Happily she watched it being taken into her grandmother's room. All was saved.

But then she began to think, Suppose Grandmother gets better? If she's changed her mind once, she could easily do it again. She did not precisely want her grandmother dead, but—well, she couldn't help remembering something Leonard had said as he saw her off for Los Angeles: "Why don't you slip something in the old bag's medicine!"

And, miraculously, opportunity presented itself. For the night nurse could not come the following evening, and no replacement was available. Shirlee-Ann volunteered to see her grandmother through the hours of darkness.

That night Shirlee-Ann gave her grandmother an overdose. As the old woman swallowed the medicine, she said: "I knew you were a good girl, Shirlee-Ann." And then she added, "I've signed the will. I put it away safe myself."

Below in the theater foyer, the clock seemed to tick all the louder. As it ticked slowly toward nine forty-five Mrs. Myers began to sink. Suddenly the silence of the old woman's bedroom was broken: "Shirlee-Ann. The will. I've cut out nephew Joseph. I've left the theater and all my money to you. After all, all that matters to me is that you are happy. Do what you will."

Downstairs the clock struck ten and Mrs. Myers' head slumped on the pillow.

Next morning Shirlee-Ann visited the Gibson attorney.

"Your grandmother did not say where the new will was placed?"

Shirlee-Ann shook her head. "No, she just told me she'd signed it and put it away safe. But how she did it, I don't know. She was bedfast. None of the nurses or theater staff knew anything about it."

"Well," continued the attorney, "I know she signed it. But unfortunately, Miss Myers, the law demands that actual documents be produced. So the earlier will cannot be set aside until the new one is found."

Leonard Banks came out from New York to help her look for the will and contest nephew Joseph's legacy. At the end of a fruitless day's searching, Shirlee-Ann noticed that the old clock in the foyer had stopped—exactly the moment of Mrs. Myers' death. At last the clock was dead, as dead as her grandmother. In a sense she had murdered it too.

In the case of the clock, however, the murder was easily undone. Shirlee-Ann felt a compulsion to prove that this was so. She wound the clock and set the pendulum aswing. The brass balance arced once or twice, but the clock stopped again. Once more Shirlee-Ann tried to start it, but it was like reanimating the dead. Leonard had a try, but he couldn't get it started either.

"Stupid old clock!" He gave it a shake. As he did so, the top of the pedestal split and collapsed with age. The heavy clock slid forward. There was a crash of weights, and the brass pendulum swung wildly. The whole thing fell on Shirlee-Ann and toppled her down the stairs onto the tiles of the foyer.

Leonard Banks raced down the stairs. All his efforts to revive Shirlee-Ann were hopeless. She was dead, killed by the clock.

It was some little time before Leonard—or the theater staff, who had quickly gathered on hearing the noise—saw the long legal envelope lying in an angle on the stairs. It had been wedged under the clock, putting it off balance and preventing it from working properly. The envelope contained the will.

The Gibson family attorney informed Leonard Banks after the inquest on Shirlee-Ann's death that the will had named Shirlee-Ann sole heir. As her husband, he could have had some claim on her estate. As her fiancé, he was entitled to nothing.

A yellowing newspaper cutting can be added to the data on the Primrose Theater, Los Angeles:

> Dateline, Los Angeles. Ernl Warburg reporting.
>
> The recent demolition of the Primrose Theatre will stir the memories of older Los Angeles folks. . . . In the late years of the theater it was famous for its ghostly Grey Lady who used to hover near an old clock at the top of the foyer steps. . . .

CHAPTER 5

London's Haunted Theaterland

In all there are about twenty haunted theaters in London's theaterland. Most of the buildings where psychic happenings took place have been demolished; nevertheless their ghosts live in the folklore of the London theater.

Adelphi Theatre, Strand

The Adelphi is a district south of London's famous Strand, and it derived its name from *adelphoi* (Greek for "brothers") because its development was due to Robert Adam and his brothers James and William. Originally there was a theater here called the Sans Pareil, which opened on November 27, 1806, but it was given its present name in 1819. This playhouse had a checkered career, yet it won fame with the presentation of the "Adelphi melodramas" of Madame Céleste and Ben Webster of 1844 and Gatti from 1879: The profits from the plays allowed the theater to be rebuilt in 1858.

A much-loved Victorian actor, William Terriss—father of actress Ellaline Terriss and father-in-law to the late actor Sir Seymour Hicks—was the idol at the Adelphi for many years. The theater world was shocked when William Terriss was stabbed to death by a mad actor, Richard Archer Prince, over an imaginary grievance on December 16, 1897. Thereafter the theater was considered haunted by Terriss' ghost.

One recorded sighting dates back to 1928. The psychic investigator Joseph Braddock left a note on this ghost in 1956:

A man, who at the time had never heard of the murder, was walking in the narrow shadowy alley alongside the Adelphi Theatre. Suddenly he stared hard because he had seen a handsome old-fashioned figure pass him oddly dressed, with a flowing tie and a sombrero hat. The man was surprised and turned round to have another look, but the alley was empty and there had not been time for any living person to disappear. The man, who had never believed in ghosts, when told the facts of the murder, became convinced that he had seen the ghost of Terriss, particularly as the apparition must have vanished near the door through which the actor had so often entered the theatre, the last time to die.

Some years afterward, the *Sunday Dispatch* (January 15, 1956) ran the story that in November 1955 the ghost of William Terriss had been seen in Covent Garden Underground Station by several members of the station staff:

A four-page report was sent to the London Transport Executive divisional headquarters concerning the statuesque figure of a man wearing a grey suit, old-fashioned collar and white gloves. . . . Foreman Collector Jack Hayden, one of those who saw this tall distinguished-looking spectre more than once, eventually rang headquarters at Leicester Square: "We have a ghost here," he said. Foreman Eric Davey, a Spiritualist, was sent down and held a séance in the ante-room. Davèy said: "I got the name T-E-R . . . Something and a murder nearby. That evening somebody suggested Terriss." Pictures of the actor were found. They resembled a psychic sketch made by Davey. "That's him," Hayden said.

The ghost was seen again in 1962 by theater staff. Yet for over seventy years the theater has been the scene of strange lights, odd rapping noises, and tappings which all emanate from the dressing rooms used by Terriss. These unexplained noises have puzzled many actors and actresses. Why should they occur? Then one old bit-part actor, Charles Faversham, remembered: "I was a scene-shifter when old Terriss was murdered in Maiden Lane by Prince, and I saw them carry his bleeding body in; I can see it now, his leading-lady Jessie Milward cradled him in her arms and he died there twenty minutes later. Now every time he went out he had the habit of tapping a couple of times with his stick on the door of Miss Milward's dressing room, just to let her know he was away."

June, the well-known musical comedy actress, experienced the tappings in March, 1928. A chaise longue was also levitated in her dressing room, and she saw for some seconds a greenish light hovering in front of the mirror. Her sightings of the manifestations were to be unique, however, for she felt "something" grip her forearm, and later painful weals appeared on the arm. June's dresser, Ethel Rollin, also heard the tappings.

No psychic happenings are recorded, it seems, regarding William Terriss' murderer. Prince was found guilty but insane and spent the rest of his life in Broadmoor, an institution for the criminally insane, where he died in 1937, aged seventy-one.

Ivor Novello (1893–1951), composer of "Keep the Home Fires Burning" and author-composer of the plays *Glamorous Night* and *King's Rhapsody*, among other pieces, is thought to haunt the Adelphi, where he had many successes. That is, his wraith is there when it's not haunting the Palace Theatre in Cambridge Circus, where he was seen in 1973–74 by actor Peter Wyngarde, then starring in *The King and I*. Mr. Wyngarde reported that the ghost "used to steal things."

No one really knows how many ghosts haunt the Adelphi or whether or not it is one ghost masquerading as three—Terriss, Novello, and maybe even Charles Kean (1811–1868). Not all the psychic phenomena here are the same. Noises, lights, and ghostly emanations do not always coincide. All that one theater electrician saw, for instance, late one night, was a phantom in a gray suit silently walking through a whole row of seats—tipping them up as he went—then disappear through the wall near a door marked "Exit."

Coliseum Theatre, St. Martin's Lane

Named after the famous Colosseum in Rome, the Coliseum has only been haunted, it seems, by one ghost. Along with a host of young soldiers, one subaltern—a junior officer—in 1918 made a last visit to see the high-kicking chorus of the Coliseum before embarking for the Western Front. The night that this subaltern led his men toward the enemy lines— October 3, 1918—his ghost was seen in the theater. The soldier was killed and his uniformed remains recognized. But even as his mortal body lay dead in the Flanders mud, at the Coliseum Theatre in London, his ghost slowly made its way down the rows of seats of the dress circle. Only minutes before the house lights dimmed, the ghost took his seat two rows from the front.

During the years between the two World Wars, the ghost of the khaki-clad soldier was seen mostly in the auditorium. Emma Martin remembers:

> I was sitting in the dress circle with my father, Harry Martin, the impresario. It must have been around the 19th October, as I remember the papers saying that the Germans had been driven back from Zeebrugge and Bruges. Just as the lights in the theatre were dimmed this soldier hurried down the aisle and sat two rows in front of us in the last available seat. I recall seeing his head being silhouetted against the stage lights, then I was taken up by the action on stage, and when I looked again he had gone; in the meantime, of course, no one had passed us. Father said that the soldier's flashes [insignia] were of a cavalry regiment.

There are no recent sightings of the revenant.

Collins Music Hall, Islington Green

This music hall was demolished several years ago following a devastating fire; memories of its ghost, however, remain with such performers as Marie Lloyd, Little Tich, and Harry Randall. The specter, folk say, was that of an Irishman called Vagg, who toured the vaudeville theaters of Britain as Sam Collins: The Singing Chimney Sweep. This ghost had haunted the theater for a number of years before its final curtain fell in 1963, and it materialized usually around 9 P.M. in the manager's office. Before and during the manifestation, doors would slam shut of their own accord, even when they had been jammed open with pieces of metal. Small desk items like paper clips, a cigarette lighter, and so on would be levitated; at least this is what the theater's proprietor, Lew Lake, attested to in 1948.

Once someone accepted a challenge to sleep overnight on the couch in the manager's office, but the man fled when he felt an icy phantom grasp on his neck. Archie Bowles, who was a cleaner at the theater for a number of years, said: "More than once I was tidying out the governor's office when a knock would come to the door and a terrible rattling of the doorknob. There was never anyone there when I answered: the knock always seemed to coincide with the interval during the second performance."

This theater was also said to be haunted by the ghost of Dan Leno. The wraith would turn up at rehearsals—occupying the same seat in the stalls—and indulge in the mortal habit Leno had of snapping his fingers during a bad performance. Testimony of this was left by Chris Rowlands, who was stage manager at the Collins for forty years.

Grand Theatre, Fulham

The Grand Theatre at Fulham stood in Putney Bridge Approach, so near to the River Thames that the stalls were under water every time the river overflowed. The theater was built by the former business manager of the spookless Criterion Theatre, Alex F. Henderson (1866–1933), and was opened on August 23, 1897, with a production of *The Geisha*.

Once 2,239 people could watch a show at any one time and gave resounding welcomes to such favorites as Charles Warner, John Hare, Charles Wyndham, and the legendary Sarah Bernhardt. According to an old actress who now lives in one of the retired-thespians homes, the theater was haunted by a Miss East Robertson, who once, during a performance of *A Woman's Pluck*, caused a sensation by starring as a lady pugilist. Miss Robinson's ghost appeared here apparently in the 1920's and was remembered by the actress Violet Vanbrugh as being "draped in furs."

A relative of East Robertson, John M. East, an actor-manager who managed the theater from 1892 to 1904, was said to haunt the Lyric at Hammersmith. The ghost was audible, complaining about the drudgery of the people who once lived here and whom, in life, he had attempted to entertain.

Renamed the Fulham Theatre in 1906, the playhouse was demolished in 1958.

Haymarket Theatre, West End

Built on the site of John Potter's Little-Theatre-in-the-Hay of 1720—which eventually became London's third Theatre Royal—the present Haymarket Theatre, built by John Nash, opened its doors in 1821. Its ghost is said to be that of John Baldwin Buckstone, an old actor-manager who was here from 1853 to 1879, who died "of a broken heart" during his tenancy of the theater. He is hardly ever seen, only heard. According to eyewitnesses the door of his old dressing room opens, and footsteps cross the floor to a cupboard, then recede, and the door again closes. Mrs. Stuart Watson, the chairman and managing director of the theater, has often seen Buckstone: "He is not a misty figure, and you can't see through him. He looks real flesh and blood."

Actor Stringer Davis and his wife, actress Margaret Rutherford, shared a psychic experience at the Haymarket Theatre. Once, during a railway strike, Margaret Rutherford reported to startled newsmen, she and Stringer "camped out" overnight at the Haymarket when they were appearing in *The School for Scandal*. Their dressing room had a bricked-up door that used to give access to the stage. Next to it was the costume wardrobe, where Margaret also stored drinks for her guests. On this particular night, Miss Rutherford said, she had a most vivid dream:

"I had gone to the cupboard in my dream—the action of which was very, very real to me—and I couldn't get the door shut because of the voluminousness of my dresses. Amid them I saw a man's hairy leg and caught a glimpse of his face. Without a doubt it was the face of John Buckstone—I remember once seeing a portrait of him, but never associated him with the Haymarket."

She awoke with a sense of elation and told Stringer Davis of her dream. He said that, as Margaret had called out and roused him in his sleep, he heard the cupboard door creak and the bottles rattle inside. "It seemed our joint experiences set the seal of validity on them," concluded Margaret Rutherford. The following evening it appears that Miss Rutherford and her dresser thought they caught a glimpse of John Buckstone entering the room.

In a report in *The Star* for April 29, 1944, the actress Drusilla Willis, who was appearing in *Yellow Sands*, saw Buckstone's wraith backstage. The actor Victor Leslie once returned to his dressing room at the theater to find an "elderly man in an old-fashioned suit" declaiming Shakespeare in his armchair. Indignant, Leslie locked the door—there was only one way out—and went for the stage manager. On returning the two men found the room empty, except for an apparently apported, old account book, which mysteriously appeared on the chair where the ghost had been sitting.

From time to time Buckstone has appeared not only in a box but on stage. One Haymarket buff remembers:

> In 1963, when the late Michael Flanders was appearing in the review *At the Drop of a Hat*, the assistant stage manager saw a man standing behind the performer's wheelchair. [Flanders was a polio victim]. Thinking that it must be a stagehand who had been trapped on stage when the curtain went up, the stage manager was about to give instructions for the curtain to be lowered when the figure moved and it was seen that it could not be a stagehand since the figure was dressed in a long black frock-coat. As the stage manager watched, very puzzled as to who the man could be, the figure suddenly vanished midstage. A description of the figure admirably fitted John Buckstone.

Some say that the Haymarket is also haunted by David Edward Morris, a former partner-manager; his materializations were commented upon by eyewitnesses, including Frederick Harrison (manager 1896–1926) and business manager Horace Watson. Mrs. Stuart Watson also avers that the theater is haunted by Henry Fielding (1707–54), the celebrated English author of the novel *Tom Jones*.

London Palladium, Argyll Street

On the site where the famous London Palladium now stands was the town house—Argyll House—that belonged to the Dukes of Argyll. At the rear of the theater's royal circle there exists the old Crimson Staircase, which is said to be a remnant of the ducal house. Down this staircase, from time to time, comes the ghost of a crinolined lady. She has been seen by staff, audience, artists, and music-hall stars. She makes no sound; not even the rustling of her gown can be heard.

The ghostly woman is thought to be the spirit of Helen Campbell, a kinswoman of George John Douglas Campbell (1823–1900), Eighth Duke of Argyll, who was a well-known Liberal Member of Parliament. She was continuously grieving for the historic wrongs wrought on fellow Scots by the powerful Campbell family. In life she threatened to haunt, when dead, Campbell property as a personal penance.

Lyceum Theatre, Wellington Street

From 1871 to 1902 this theater was the home of Sir Henry Irving's company, and the scene of his and Ellen Terry's greatest triumphs. The site had been used as a theater since 1772, but was latterly to become a dance hall. In the 1900's the old building was demolished, leaving only the Corinthian portico.

During the 1880's a strange psychic occurrence took place at the Lyceum. A man and his wife, who occupied one of the boxes, were chatting to each other during the first interval, when the man's gaze became fastened on a woman, wearing flowing silks, sitting in the fourth row of the stalls, about the twelfth seat along. Could he believe his eyes? Was that a man's head in the woman's lap? Yes, his wife confirmed the fact just as the lights were going down.

To satisfy their curiosity, during the next interval the man and his wife went down to the stalls to get a closer look. They couldn't get near enough, but saw that the object was now covered by a silk wrap on the woman's lap. They returned to their box, and at the end of the play they tried to intercept the woman but missed her in the crowd. However, the face of the head remained fixed in their memories. It belonged to a person of the cavalier type, with long hair, moustache, and pointed beard—it looked pallid, dead, and as if it had just come off at an execution.

This grisly event passed from the man's memory until

some years later, when he traveled to Yorkshire to value some old paintings at Temple Newsam, near Leeds. In a stockroom he found two portraits, on the wrapper of which was a label saying that they had once hung at the Lyceum Theatre. As he unwrapped the paper and looked at the paintings, the art collector had a shock, for one of the paintings was of the man whose head he had seen in the woman's lap all those years before.

Making inquiries, the collector found that the two paintings were of members of the family of the Earls of Essex. One of this family was beheaded in the early days of Oliver Cromwell's rule. The Essex family had once owned the ground on which the Lyceum was built. It may be doubted that the woman in the stalls of the Lyceum was aware of the gruesome burden in her lap.

It is on record too that a corpselike figure used to stalk backstage during performances.

Marlborough Theatre, Holloway

Long replaced, this theatre was once haunted by an irritable old actor's ghost. Grumbling to itself, the specter would stamp near the vicinity of the manager's office, fingering its astrakhan collar. A former manager of the theater, Billy Quest, was often told by patrons and artists that they had seen the ghost, but he never saw it himself.

Every psychic researcher hopes that he can come across a unique story for his collection. One such concerns Helen Shaftesbury, a character actress who played the Marlborough during 1896–1902.

During the summer of 1900, Helen Shaftesbury spent a vacation with the Warrens of Layer-de-la-Haye, Essex. At the time she was collecting notes for a paper on the use of the picture of Saint Christopher in Essex churches. At one time most churches in the country had a picture of this saint on the north wall by the door, where all might see it as they came out of church and ask the saint's protection on their everyday travels. Miss Shaftesbury noted the Saint Christophers at Little Baddow, Canewdon, Feering, Ingatestone, Latton, Fairsted, and Ongar, and at last cycled over to see the one at St. Mary's Layer Marney.

The Layer Marney Saint Christopher is hung, most unusually, at the east end of the nave and was somewhat "renovated" in the 1880's. Yet the honest-to-goodness face of the saint was appealing, and Miss Shaftesbury set up her small easel to take a pencil likeness of the old, big-featured man with the eel twisted around one ankle, to hang in her dressing room.

She had almost finished her preliminary sketch of the Saint Christopher picture when a rustling sound behind her attracted her attention. As she turned around, she heard a voice softly say, "Marney." Miss Shaftesbury listened for a moment, heard nothing more, and continued with her work. A few minutes later the rustling sound was heard again and the gentle voice calling, "Marney." This time Miss Shaftesbury got up from her camp stool and looked around the church. There was nothing unusual, and no one to be seen. She was quite alone.

About ten minutes later the exact thing happened again. Getting a little annoyed and thinking someone was playing a trick on her, the actress jumped up and said, "Who's there? What do you want?" in a loud voice and with as much authority as she could muster. There was no answer. On returning to her stool her attention was drawn to a monument bearing the inscription "Sir Henry, First Lord Marney."

Intrigued, Miss Shaftesbury searched around the church to see if she could find any further inscriptions about the Marney family, of whom she had never heard. Finding nothing, she called at the vicarage when she had completed her picture. The vicar was out, but his wife offered her a cup of tea and an invitation to "look up" Sir Henry in her husband's library.

As the clock on the mantelpiece ticked away, the actress began to build up a picture of the Tudor gentleman from the dusty books. Sir Henry had been the son of Sir John Marney of Layer Marney and his wife, Jane Throckmorton. Born in 1457, Sir Henry had been a Privy Councillor to King Henry VII in 1485 and had fought at the Battle of Stoke in 1487, and the Battle of Blackheath. In 1494 he was created a knight bachelor, and from 1509 until his death was chancellor of the Duchy of Lancaster. Under King Henry VIII he held various positions, including Keeper of the Privy Seal. On April 9, 1523, the King created him Baron Marney at Richmond. Sir Henry was married twice, first to Thomazine Arundell of Cornwall, and secondly to Elizabeth Wyfold of Holloway, London. How strange, thought the actress, the very district I am playing at the moment!

The distinguished man died on May 24, 1523, at his house in St. Swithen's Lane, London. His body was brought back to Layer Marney church, where he was buried in the chancel —Miss Shaftesbury noted that this was from where she thought the mystery voice had appeared to emanate.

A benefactor to his county and the builder of an almshouse, Sir Henry had ordered the erection of Layer Marney Tower at Tiptree. The edifice had been started in 1517 but was never finished. Today the building remains not a mansion but an enormous gateway rivaling that of Thomas Cardinal Wolsey's at the palace of Hampton Court. Layer Marney Tower, with its distinctive black bricks, has two large eight-story octagonal towers, flanking two central stories all lighted with small pointed windows. There it was in 1798 that a group of wandering players, rehearsing for a harvest-festival play, had been terrified by the voice of a ghost repeating the name "Marney." Sir Henry certainly had a penchant for actors.

Just as she finished reading, the vicar returned, and Miss Shaftesbury told him about the mysterious voice in the church. The clergyman was silent for a while and then said,

"Several of my parishioners have heard a voice in the church calling out Marney, but on most occasions it has been around the anniversary of Sir Henry's death, say at Easter or early May." Every time the voice had been heard, someone had been looking at the Saint Christopher picture, just as the actress had done. This had led to its nickname "Sir Henry's favorite picture."

The vicar told Helen Shaftesbury that his predecessor had actually seen Sir Henry's wraith walking down the chancel away from the picture and had met two people who had also seen and heard the ghost, but this time at Layer Marney Tower itself. Sometime around the early 1860's, two workmen had been doing some repair work in the top room of one of the towers of the building. Since the work had to be completed within a certain time limit, the workmen had taken bedrolls and camped out nearby.

Three nights they spent in a turret room at Layer Marney Tower, and each night their slumbers were interrupted by the banging of a door—as if it were being continually slammed shut. Getting up to investigate the noise, the workmen located the door that must have been slammed. They found, however, that it was heavily bolted and the hinges and fastenings were so rusted that no one could have opened it without damaging the woodwork.

On the third night the men had been roused again, but as they approached the door, they saw the figure of a man in armor standing by the portal. Around the specter's shoulders was swathed a cloak and in his hand he carried a large seal. Some time afterward, one of the men said that the figure they had seen greatly resembled the recumbent figure among the Marney Tombs at Layer Marney church.

The room where the workmen were was the same as that in which the actors had heard the manifestation.

Helen Shaftesbury wrote an account of the ghost in her diary and of her conversation with the vicar. She wrote: "I heard the voice in the church clearly three times within a matter of minutes. It was a deep, rather guttural voice with a rather countrified accent. Never before this had I heard the surname Marney mentioned nor had I heard of Sir Henry before."

Miss Shaftesbury's diary was found among her papers on her death in 1928. For devotees of the theater ghost, the journal is particularly interesting because under the date February 17, 1901, is this fascinating entry:

> Sir Henry followed me to the Marlborough. It so happened that in the early months of the year we were doing a play with knights in armour in it. Before every performance, the name Marney was heard to echo round the theatre. In the same accent I had heard before. Was it on the site of the theatre that Sir Henry's second wife had lived, and through me he had come back from Essex to find her?

A séance was held at the theater, and during the vigil the name "Marney" was spoken. But this time the voice said, "Pity poor Bett." Was it referring to Elizabeth Wyfold of Holloway?

Metropolitan Music Hall, Edgeware Road

Now demolished, this vaudeville theater had a ghost that was deemed to be the spirit of a former manager who had been killed during active service in World War I. He was often seen by artists, watching the stage and the house. When the audience was sparse, the ghost, dressed in a brown suit, would walk up and down, very agitated.

New Theatre, St. Martin's Lane

This theater (now the Albery Theatre) was built for Sir Charles Wyndham (1837–1919) and his wife, Mary Moore, whose son by her first marriage, Sir Bronson Albery, controlled it until his death in 1971. One day, it appears, the well-known actor Barry Jones was sitting on some backstage steps of the theater during a break in rehearsal. A rather handsome man with wavy gray hair suddenly appeared behind him. Thinking that the man wanted to pass, Jones and the actress he was talking to both stood aside. The man nodded his thanks as he passed, and crossing the stage went toward the dressing rooms.

A few minutes later the man's appearance struck a chord in Barry Jones's memory. He went over to where the man had vanished and, finding an attendant standing by the door the man must have gone through, Jones asked if he had noticed anyone pass. The man was definite that he had seen no one. Jones and the actress were just as definite that they had seen the gray-haired man, whom Jones now remembered. It had been Sir Charles Wyndham. But Sir Charles had been dead for years.

Old Royalty

A woman dressed in a white gown of Queen Anne's reign (1702–1714) is said to have been seen at this theater before it was destroyed. W. Macqueen Pope records having seen the ghost of "an old lady" here.

Old Vic, Waterloo Road

This theater was opened on May 11, 1818, as the Royal Coburg Theatre. Its name was later changed to the Royal Victoria Theatre in honor of Queen Victoria. Once it was known for "sensational melodrama with a rough unmannerly audience," but it was to win fame as a "Shakespearean theatre" inspired by Lilian Baylis. Not surprisingly, the ghost of the Old Vic combines both the blood-and-thunder and Shakespearean aspects of the theater's history. From time to time a frightful specter of a distraught woman, wringing her bloodstained hands, appears, reenacting the part of Lady Macbeth.

Grampian Theatre, Shaftesbury Avenue

In a letter to my late grandfather, "Britain's best-known ghost hunter," the late Elliott O'Donnell, told of a theater mystery that had been recounted to him during a tour in 1899 by a relative of the actress concerned. The Grampian Theatre is no more, but, like many other small theaters, it changed its name many times during its history. This is the story as it was taken from the psychic Elliott O'Donnell's holograph letter of December 31, 1927:

One evening at about half past six, actress Connie Burton entered the backstage area of the Grampian Theatre, where she was appearing in *The Brigands*, and ascended the stone staircase to the dressing room she shared with several other chorus girls. As she reached the passage leading to the chorus dressing room, she saw her friend Sonia Lester standing at the door of her own dressing room. Sonia glanced at her with a troubled expression, and Connie wanted to stop and talk to her, for she knew that worries had been piling up on the other girl recently. But she was late, so she postponed the talk. As she hurried down the passage, she saw Sonia turn the handle, open the dressing-room door, slip inside, and close the door behind her. Then Connie rather forgot the other girl in the bustle of getting ready to go on stage herself.

Connie just managed to be on stage in time for the overture. Sonia wasn't there yet, but her entrance was not until the first scene of the second act, so Connie thought nothing of it. As the first-act curtain was about to go up, another chorus girl asked if she had seen Sonia, and she answered yes.

"Well, she wasn't in her room just now when I went there

with a message from Mr. Clements," the girl replied. Mr. Clements was the producer.

There was no time for further conversation, but Sonia did not appear backstage at any time during the first act.

Shortly before the curtain rose for the second act, Clements was in the wings, talking to the stage manager and anxiously waiting to speak to Sonia. There was no sign of her.

"I hope nothing is the matter with her," he said to the stage manager. "I am getting worried. I was told she was not at all well last night. Just now I sent someone to her room to inquire, but she was not there, and that's rather strange, for she should have been dressing."

"Very likely she was in someone else's room," the stage manager suggested. "I was talking to Joe at the stage door tonight when she came in. I thought she looked rather pale, but otherwise she seemed quite her usual self."

Clements grew more and more fidgety. All the other actors in that scene were either in their places on the stage or in the wings ready to go on, and still no Sonia. He gave orders for the curtain to be held till he found out what was keeping her and sent someone to her room to find her. Still Sonia was not there. What to do? The curtain could not be kept back much longer. The audience was already getting restless, shuffling its feet and murmuring.

The producer gave up and sent for Sonia's understudy, and the show continued.

But that didn't answer the question of what had happened to Sonia. Much worried now, for the girl was a favorite with him as she was with nearly all the company, Clements instituted a search for her. She was nowhere to be found. He interviewed Joe Peal, the stage doorman, and Peal corroborated what the stage manager had told him.

"I saw her, Mr. Clements," he said, "as clearly as I see you now. It was Miss Lester right enough. She came as usual at half-past six. I was rather surprised that she didn't say something to me, as she always does. She went by as if she was in a hurry, looking neither to the right nor left."

"Did she look as if there was anything the matter with her?" Clements asked.

The doorman shook his head. "She looked rather white and as if something was troubling her, but apart from that, she seemed quite her usual self."

"Did you see her leave?"

The doorman thought a moment. "Now I come to think of it," he said slowly, "I didn't. Had she passed my office, I must have seen her—the door was wide open. But I am positive she never went by."

Clements was puzzled. "I can't understand it," he muttered. "Where the devil can she be?"

He questioned the members of the cast. Connie Burton was apparently the only one who had seen her.

"I take my oath it was Sonia," she insisted. "I saw her standing in the passage outside her room, with one hand on the door handle. I was only a few feet from her. I could almost have touched her. She didn't speak, only turned her head, looked at me, and then went into her room. If I hadn't been in such a hurry, I would have spoken to her."

"Did she look ill?" Clements asked.

"She didn't look any too grand," Connie said, "but she hasn't for the last few days. Her eyes have been bothering her. She was going to see a specialist about them this morning."

Sonia's part in the show being only a very minor one, she did not have a dresser. Otherwise a dresser's testimony would have been of great importance, as would that of the girl who usually shared Sonia's room; unfortunately the latter was away that night with a bad cold. The call boy was of no help; he couldn't remember whether he heard anyone in the room, when he knocked at the door, or not. Sonia's presence at the theater that night rested solely on the testimony of Joe the stage doorman, the stage manager, and Connie Burton, and all three insisted that they had seen her there.

Sorely puzzled, Clements drove to Sonia's flat. Mary Lester, Sonia's sister, opened the door to him, red-eyed and pale.

"I hope there's nothing the matter with your sister," he said.

"Then you don't know," she cried. "I thought you must somehow have heard."

A chill feeling of apprehension ran through him. "Know what?"

"Sonia is dead," Mary said in a choking voice. "She died suddenly at six thirty this evening. I ought to have let you know, but I was too upset. Her health had been bad for some time, and the worry about her eyes—she feared that she was going blind—made it worse."

Clements was shocked. He expressed his great distress and sympathy to Mary, and returned at once to the theater.

"You must have been mistaken," he said to Connie and the man at the stage door. "You could not have seen Sonia. She died at her home at six thirty this evening."

They were unshaken, however, in their conviction that it was Sonia whom they had seen that evening at six thirty. "If it was not Sonia herself," they told Clements and everyone in the theater, "it must have been her ghost."

This is the only recorded version of the ghost of Sonia Lester at the Grampian.

Royalty Theatre, Dean Street

This theater was built in 1840 by Fanny Kelly on the site of an eighteenth-century house, which itself was reported to have been haunted. The theater was erected, it is said, with money supplied by the Duke of Devonshire. Ghost hunter R. Thurston Hopkins left the best version of this haunting:

> The spectre is a gypsy girl, dressed in a vivid green and scarlet silk gown and she rattles a tambourine as she wan-

ders through the offices, which contain some of the rooms of the Queen Anne building. It is said that she makes her way down the stairs to the vestibule and vanishes. She only walks when the orchestra is playing, and it is the music of the violin (the devil's staff the gypsies call it) which attracts her, for her lover was a Romany fiddler. She is always seeking to hear the magical fire of a gypsy violin. It is said that the Romany fiddler murdered the girl and buried her in a hollow wall of the ancient house which was afterwards incorporated in the Royalty Theatre. When the theatre was erected the workmen discovered the girl's almost mummified body in a tomb of plaster of Paris.

Another ghost is associated with the theater, that of "a little old lady dressed in early Victorian costume." Most of the attendants at the Royalty saw her at one time or another as a "misty and gray form." She had a happy atmosphere about her, and she usually appeared as a performance was about to start. Many patrons saw her too—an old lady in ringlets, silk dress, and bonnet.

Sadler's Wells Theatre, Rosebery Avenue

Besides haunting the Theatre Royal, Drury Lane, the ghost of the famous clown Joseph Grimaldi also visits this theater, which goes back to the seventeenth century. On its site in 1683 a Thomas Sadler discovered a medicinal spring, and built a small "musick house" so that people might drink the waters in pleasant surroundings. There has been a theater here since Rusman's original of 1753. The theater closed, after a mixed career, in 1903 but was reopened in 1931. It suffered war damage and now presents a year-round season of opera, ballet, and drama.

Grimaldi knew the theater well—as did his show-business family, who entertained packed houses here. His ghost has been seen in one of the boxes in the dead of night, staring at the auditorium with glassy eyes. There have been occasions too when his face—in a clown's white pan makeup—has been seen behind people sitting in the box.

St. James's Theatre, King Street

Designed by Samuel Beazley and built by the singer John Braham, the St. James's opened its doors to the public on December 14, 1835. Designed with a Roman facade and an interior reflecting the theater of the Palace of Versailles, it was an "unlucky theater," even though one of its greatest performers, Sir George Alexander, brought it fame and Charles Dickens wrote a burletta (a musical comic opera), which was staged here. The theater was the home of a tactile ghost, a ghost of touch. Several people were "helped on" with coats and costumes while in a certain dressing-room. Could this have been the ghost of some earthbound dresser?

The theater was demolished in 1957. It is interesting to note that the site was once occupied by Nerot's Hotel, to which Horatio Viscount Nelson (1758–1805) returned after his victorious Battle of the Nile. The hotel was deemed haunted by the ghost of an eighteenth-century actress who once lodged there.

Theatre Royal, Angel Lane, Stratford-atte-Bow

Joan Littlewood's Theatre Workshop made this theater famous in the 1950's. Its history, however, goes back to 1880, when it was built by Freddy Fredericks, who is thought to walk the buildings' dark corridors still. Those who have seen the ghost—"a small, tubby fellow, dressed in brown"—say that he is friendly and that he comes to see that his initials FF remain in the middle of the arch spanning the stage.

Theatre Royal, Drury Lane

Undoubtedly the most famous of all London's haunted theaters.

There have been four theaters of this name on the present site. The first of 1663–72 was destroyed by fire. The second of 1674–1791 was demolished because of age and disrepair. The third of 1794–1809 was also destroyed by fire. And the present noble building was established in 1812. Thus Drury Lane, by virtue of its foundation and history, is an entity unique among the theaters of the world.

Edmund Kean, Dan Leno, Sir Frank Benson, and thousands of other famous names have played here, and a sparkling history of hits like *Rose Marie* (1925), *Cavalcade* (1931), *Glamorous Night* (1935), *Oklahoma* (1947), and *Hello Dolly* (1965) entertained packed audiences. The longest run has been achieved here, however, by the ghostly man in gray.

This ghost has been seen by hundreds of people during the last two hundred years. Yet the man who has seen it most often was the great doyen of the theater, W. Macqueen Pope. He averred that the ghost did "not behave in a manner generally accepted as conventional for spooks and spectres."

The Gray Man of Drury Lane, it seems, walks only by day; he makes no noise and walks around harming no one, in a gentlemanly way. He is purely a local ghost, and is seen in only one part of the house and always moves in the same direction in his walk—counterclockwise. The specter comes quietly out of the wall of a room on the upper circle level (now used as a bar), walks across it, through the glass door, turns left into the upper circle, ascends the stairs, walks right around the back, down the stairs on the other side, through another door, and through the wall again in the room—also a bar—which is on the opposite side of the theater to that from which he appears.

So far as can be ascertained, the ghost does not have regular days for perambulation; sometimes he is seen frequently, sometimes months elapse. He gives no warning, neither does he dislike company. He has been seen by members of the audience when a matinee was in progress and was not the least disturbed when a bomb dropped right in the middle of his walk during World War II!

Strangely enough, the ghost is a good judge of a play. He is seen most frequently during the run of a success, and does not patronize flops. Consequently, a sight of him before a new production starts is considered a good omen. He revealed himself before the first night of *Oklahoma*, two days before *Carousel*, and two days before *South Pacific*. He ignored Noel Coward's *Pacific 1860*, which flopped.

Most descriptions of him agree. He wears a wide dark-colored hat on his powdered hair or wig; his long riding cloak is draped around him, covering a dress coat with ruffled sleeves; the end of his sword can be seen and his riding boots too. It has been even possible on some occasions to glimpse his features—a strong, well-formed face, with a good chin and clear-cut nose. All in all, the general impression is the same as when one sees figures on the stage through a gauze.

No one has ever got nearer to him than forty feet or so. There is no recorded data on who the ghost was in mortal life, but he is usually associated with a strange discovery made around 1848. In a tiny room, bricked up in the thickness of the walls (those adjoining Russell Street, which are the only remaining walls of the building designed by Sir Christopher Wren), a skeleton was found with a dagger of Cromwellian pattern in its ribs. Is the ghost the wandering spirit of a man murdered in the seventeenth century in Drury Lane who was quietly bricked up? The ghost does appear from the wall adjoining where the skeleton was found. The bones, by the way, were buried in the little cemetery at the corner of Russell Street and Drury Lane, the cemetery mentioned by Dickens in *Bleak House* as the place where Lady Dedlock died.

Some people, like American actress Betty Jo Jones, who appeared in *Oklahoma*, have seen the ghost of the great clown Joseph Grimaldi (1779–1837) on stage. Seen in front of the pit sometimes is a tall, emaciated, hatchet-faced ghost whose description fits quick-tempered Irish actor Charles Macklin (1700–1797). In a quarrel over a wig, Macklin killed fellow actor Thomas Hallam in 1735 in the Green Room.

Comedian Stanley Lupino, father of screen actress Ida Lupino, also averred that he saw and spoke to the ghost of the famous Dan Leno (1860–1904) in 1923. Lupino said that he had decided to sleep in his dressing room after a show (it was a very wet and stormy night), and he had just dozed off when he had a feeling that he was not alone. He saw a shadowy form moving across the room—and a few minutes later, he recognized the materialized face of Dan Leno. Lupino's wife saw the ghost in the same room the next day and promptly fainted.

Two ladies, occupying gangway seats in the side block of the dress circle, once saw Charles Kean (1811–68, the actor-manager son of the great actor Edmund Kean) sitting watching a performance—they later recognized him from a photograph.

According to actor Tony Britton, one of the cast of the hit musical *No, No, Nanette*, there is yet another phantom that haunts the old playhouse with a vengeance. Mr. Britton relates that the wardrobe mistress and her assistant were walking along a corridor in the upstairs part of the theater when a "No Smoking" sign whistled over their heads. They turned around, but no one was in sight. The same evening Mr. Britton was attacked by the ghost in his dressing room during the intermission. His chair was pulled from under him and he only saved himself from falling by holding on to a nearby wardrobe. Later that night transistor radios were mysteriously switched on and off in the dressing rooms of other members of the cast.

CHAPTER 6

Ghosts from Provincial England

A Ghost That Congratulates

In June 1854 the Landport Hall at Portsmouth, which was to be used for meetings, assemblies, and the like, was opened on the site of the old Racquet Court next door to the White Swan public house. Not long after, one Henry Rutley arrived in Portsmouth and, after becoming licensee of the White Swan, leased the Landport Hall. Immediately he set about converting the hall into a theater; and on Monday September 29, 1856, the New Theatre Royal opened its doors. The theater remained a flourishing enterprise right up to 1874 when Rutley died.

After Rutley's death the theater became celebrated for another reason—its haunting. In *The Evening News*, Portsmouth, for Friday, October 4, 1957, the then general manager of the Theatre Royal, Michael Wide, reported that he was convinced that the theater was haunted. After sleeping for some months in a dressing room at the theater, Wide became aware of "two ghosts in the building." One he believed was the theater's founder, Henry Rutley. "As I walk along the corridor to my office, I sometimes have a feeling of great friendship, as if Mr. Rutley were patting me on the back, and saying, 'That's the stuff, old boy.' " The other ghost, he says, haunts the room next to his. "The other night, I returned to the theatre late, and saw a light on in that room—Rutley's dressing room. As I walked in to switch it off, I had a most awful creepy feeling."

Others too have experienced and reported a feeling of ghostly presences. In 1956, one hundred years to the day after the theater's opening, there was another strange occurrence. A chorus girl, returning to the Rutland Room on the third floor, found that the door would not open. She went for assistance, but none could open the door and no key to fit the lock could be found. Firemen broke in, but found that the door had been unlocked all the time.

A Suicidal Sailor

The oldest part of the Castle Theatre, Farnham, Surrey—the foyer and the section leading back toward Castle Street—date from the thirteenth century. The site was originally a granary for Farnham Castle, and today, it is said, chaff is still to be found among the foundations. Much of the early history of the property suggests that it retained its farm role for many centuries, and latterly it became outbuildings, a builder's yard, a World War I delousing center, a roller-skating rink, and finally a theater.

These buildings were converted for use as a theater in 1939. It appears that a group of strolling players had come from France—where they had been touring when the Germans caused the French to mobilize—in May 1939. The company landed at Southampton and decided to work their way back to London, playing halls and barns along the way. On reaching Farnham, they played what is now the site of the Castle Theatre (closed in 1974), and decided to set themselves up permanently in this building. Calling themselves the English Classical Players, they opened on December 5, 1939. The Farnham Repertory Company was formed in 1948.

No one knows when the Castle Theatre began to have a ghostly reputation, and there is no one left who can actually claim to have seen the ghost. But several people have reported unaccountable footsteps. On one occasion a spotlight was revolved by ghostly hands in the auditorium. Neither was the theater very popular with dogs, which seem to have had an aversion for various parts of the buildings. One of the former house managers, Miss Helen M. S. Harvey, reported experiencing a strange atmosphere of coldness and a feeling that someone unseen was present that descends on the auditorium from time to time.

The ghost who worked the spotlights and tramped the boards is affectionately and respectfully known as George. In life "George" appears to have been a sailor who lived in an apartment above the theater. On returning unexpectedly from a long sea voyage, he discovered his wife in bed with her lover. Mad with rage, he murdered the pair and afterward committed suicide by hanging himself from a rafter. The very beam can still be seen in the foyer.

A Multihaunted Theater

The Theatre Royal, Addington Street, Margate, Kent, is perhaps southern England's most haunted theater. Opened in 1874, heir to 180 years of tradition and holding slightly under two thousand patrons, this theater has been associated with many famous actors. Its most famous manager was Miss Sarah Thorne, who guided its fortunes until 1894. Something of a martinet, Sarah Thorne made her theater celebrated in the south of England, but from around 1894, the playhouse began to decline. Over the years it suffered a number of vicissitudes and was turned into a furniture store. It was reopened as a theater in 1930 and subsequently it has been in turn a cinema, a theater, and a bingo hall.

Fred Archer was probably the first to make a national story about the hauntings at the Theatre Royal, Margate. According to the local papers a progressive series of hauntings began in

1918, when the ghost of Sarah Thorne was first seen. Miss
Thorne, incidentally, is believed to have come back to protest
at the modern usage of the theater, such as bingo and other
gambling games. So frightening was her wraith to some witnesses that the police were called in to investigate, but
they found nothing untoward.

Archer says that the theater "where there is a trap-door
leading to what was a smuggler's cave" probably boasts the
most diverse psychic happenings in the theatrical world: "an
orange-coloured ball of light"; "a scream which starts backstage and seems to travel across the stage and finally exits
through the stagedoor"; and "the appearance of a ghost in one
of the boxes who draws back the curtains if they are closed."
The latter phenomenon was witnessed by Macqueen Pope,
who believed this specter to be an actor who had committed
suicide by throwing himself from the box into the orchestra
pit sometime in the early 1900's. Joseph Braddock dates the
suicide to late Georgian or early Victorian times:

> An actor from a company playing at the theatre was dis-
> missed for some reason, and on the next evening he bought
> himself a box for the performance. During the course of the
> play he committed suicide by throwing himself out of the
> box into the orchestra pit. Some time during the first decade
> of our century the wraith of a man was seen sitting in the
> box so often that the management was obliged to withdraw
> the box from sale, leaving it permanently curtained, until
> finally it was bricked up.

This, however, would predate the building of the Theatre
Royal on the Addington Street site. Alternatively, the story as
Braddock heard it could have referred to the eighteenth-
century site of Margate's theater tradition, and was perhaps a
transference of the myth.

Modern testimony of the theater's hauntings comes from
Alfred Charles Tanner, who was interviewed about his sight-

ings in 1966 by Dr. A. R. G. Owen, the distinguished Cambridge parapsychologist, and Victor Sims.

Tanner, it appears, was working during January 1966 on the redecoration of the Theatre Royal when he encountered the ghostly happenings. In order that the redecoration should not interrupt the daytime bingo, Tanner had agreed to work through the night. His first night's work passed without incident, but during his second work stint he heard a series of sounds coming from the stage—as if someone were whispering. He stopped work for a few minutes to investigate, but could find no reason for the noises. Working on, he heard the natural creakings of the floorboards. Then, however, he heard the sounds of footsteps just in front of the stage and moving toward him.

As he turned around to see who was there, the footsteps stopped. No one was to be seen. Suddenly, testifies Tanner, he heard the door of the box office bang violently. Again no one was to be seen. The decorator was entirely alone in the old theater. Tanner resumed painting in the hope that the unusual noises he had heard were "natural." Just as he was getting himself calm again, the phantom footsteps started once more. They came up behind him and halted when he turned. But this time there was something more eerie. Tanner heard an extremely heavy thump on the floor between the front row of seats and the stage—as though a heavy object had fallen there. Charles Tanner looked across at the spot: "I swear I saw the dust rising, just as it would if a real object had hit the carpet." Of course no object was visible, but could this have been the materialized impact of the ghostly suicide's cadaver hitting the floor?

On the following night, Tanner was at work again when he was interrupted once more. This time he saw "a semi-transparent globular object measuring about ten inches across" moving across the stage from left to right. The globe latterly formed the shape of a head before it disappeared. This time Tanner saw curtains by the exit door being moved by an unseen hand.

The next working night Charles Tanner, who now had an assistant, Lawrence Rodgers, was haunted again. Both heard a curious bang from the dress circle. This time the police were called, but no intruders were found.

Certain aspects of these hauntings—the slow movement of the curtains and the bangs and footfalls—are typical of poltergeists, as set down by parapsychologists A. R. G. Owen and Raymond Bayliss. But the "face" remains more of an unaccounted mystery.

Following the theories of G. W. Lambert, some persons have said that the "ghostly noises" had something to do with seismic disturbances. But can earthquakes cause localization of phenomena in the theater at Margate? Can it localize noises to one position only within a building? Hardly.

Certainly the ghosts at the Theatre Royal, Margate, are best explained as poltergeists, with hallucination as a side effect in the case of the curtains and the "face"—almost as a form of mediumistic talent in terror. Above all the "atmosphere" of this theater seems to be the most charged in Britain for psychic happenings.

Lady in a Gray Dress

It is not long after they take up their duties that the managers of the Theatre Royal, Bath, Somerset, become aware of their resident ghost—a specter that consorts with the poltergeist from the pub next door. During the 1700's the old Garricks Head hotel was a gambling den, then run by the famous dandy Richard "Beau" Nash (1674–1762). The hotel was connected with the Theatre Royal by a secret passage, which acted as a quick retreat for the impecunious bucks who could not pay their debts. The hotel ghost is a heavily built man in a dark-colored wig, which matches his period costume. He disappears into the secret passage, leaving behind the aroma of toilet water.

Just through the walls is the ghostly lady in gray, who still walks, it is said, the Lower Circle corridors of the theater and sometimes occupies one of the stage boxes or a box at the rear of the Lower Circle. She is an unknown woman who committed suicide by throwing herself from the window of a room above the bar. This ghost has been seen many times by both artists and audience. Once, when a grandfather clock mistakenly chimed in the middle of a scene, she was blamed. Certainly these two ghosts overlap each other's territory, but they seem to cohabit quite amicably.

Tradition has it that the ghosts become most active when their respective premises are under new management—when the hotel gets a new landlord and the theater a new manager. When the hotel changed landlords in the 1960's, the *Bristol Evening Post* interviewed the new tenant:

> "The first day here my keys vanished. Then they turned up in the middle of the lounge floor. It is a large bunch of keys and quite impossible for them to have been there all the time.
>
> "I am not a fanciful man, but every time I go down into the cellars I can feel something, a sort of presence. It's spine-chilling.
>
> "I don't mind having a ghost in the house but the tricks he plays are annoying. He stole the mallet with which I drive the bungs into barrels, literally from behind my back. It weighs several hundred pounds but just disappeared into thin air. It was several days before I found it again."

The landlord's wife also added her testimony:

> "I do not really believe in such things as ghosts, but such odd things happen in this place. There are noises on the stairs and noises in the attic no one can explain.

"Since we have been here my baby has been waking
every morning at 3 A.M. Something disturbs her. She does
not cry, but grumbles to herself for twenty minutes and then
goes to sleep again."

Both the landlord and his wife wish that their ghost would
go and live with his lady friend at the theater. One teenage
repertory actress, when staying at the Garricks Head, reported that during the evening of her first night in the hotel,
someone knocked at her room door. She called, "Come in,"
and the door handle immediately began to turn. But there was
no one there. "It was very scary," she said later. "I was with
another girl and we were both terrified."

This actress and other guests were later awakened by a
rumbling ghostly laugh around 3 A.M. one morning: "We were
all sleeping in different rooms and we all woke and went into
the passage to listen. There was nothing imaginary about it."
On a further occasion the actress woke to find her room "filled
with a strange glow." When she put on the light, the glow
vanished.

A Liking for Violence

It was not until around World War I that the silent film
shows began to oust the music halls from popularity. In the
north of England Randall Williams was one of the original
pioneers, and his Bioscope Show caused a sensation when it
made its first appearance at Hull Fair in October 1896. From
this date the bioscope began to take the place of the dioramas
in the fairgrounds, and cinema circuits began to be developed.

Remembering one cinema in County Durham, G. L. Mellor
has said:

The Askew Picture House in Gateshead was first licensed
in 1913 by Cecil Horn . . . and a member of his family was

licensee until the cinema closed down in 1955. It was always known locally as 'Horn's' and in the silent days was "twinned" with Shipcote in Durham Road. Reels of film were carried between these two cinemas by "runners" whose wages were 8d per night, plus 4d tram fare. The manager of the Askew at this time was Dennis Eadie, an engraver by trade, who painted the attractive colour slides which were shown between the reels of film.

One of these "runners" was the late Joseph Harrap, a spiritualist, who with a fellow-spiritualist, Charles Marshall, investigated the hauntings in the Askew Picture House during 1914–1915.

Charles Marshall was rather doubtful that the manager, Dennis Eadie, would give permission for an investigation; but after some hesitation on Eadie's part the two men finally obtained it. Subsequently Marshall and Harrap went to the cinema at 11 P.M. one October night in 1914, and were let in by the nightwatchman. After questioning the nightwatchman who "heard things here that are hard to believe," the two men chose seats in the middle of the auditorium and settled down to their eerie vigil.

Later the two men reported a cold, dank, evil feeling as one o'clock approached. As the minutes went by, they heard certain creakings and jarrings, which they attributed to natural causes. Just after two o'clock they sensed "presences" all around them. The auditorium seemed to fill with invisible beings. Gradually something began to form on the bare stage, just in front of the blank screen. Very slowly "that something" on the stage took shape. Both men testified separately at their local spiritualist church that they saw the fantastically dressed figure of a girl—her head was crowned with the weird head of some animal, which looked like a bat. On her shoulders were wings. A strange light surrounded her as she fleetingly danced a grotesque gavotte on the stage.

The girl's face remained hidden by a half-mask so that

neither Harrap nor Marshall could distinguish it. Her dance ended abruptly, and the girl disappeared, as if she had passed through the screen. Her place was taken by two spectral figures of men fighting some kind of duel. They too were enveloped in the ghostly light. Suddenly Marshall nudged Harrap's arm, for in the seats nearest the stage he saw the startlingly white face of a clown watching the duelers. With the clown was another girl, dark-haired, in whose eyes was the glinting expression of the most deadly hatred that the two men had ever seen. In one hand the girl held what appeared to be a pistol; leveling it at one of the ghostly duelers on stage, she fired. Marshall and Harrap heard the shot and watched the phantoms slowly vanish.

Both men took some time to recover from the shock of what they had seen. Later they were able to compare notes with the nightwatchman, who had seen the enactment on two previous occasions but not in such vivid detail. The intensity of the two spiritualists' experience can probably be accounted for by their latent psychic potential for mediumship. Two or three days later Harrap and Marshall met Dennis Eadie and told him what they had seen. Until this time Eadie had remained skeptical of the two men's vigil; now he was profoundly interested.

"Some fifteen years ago," said Eadie, "there was an amateur theatrical group who put on plays in this very building. One play I heard tell was called *Vengeance of the Bat*. The principals were Harold Carter from Gosforth, Peter Ellis, Dolly Baker and Vera Hepple from Gateshead, and Bill Darwin from Jesmond. Harold Carter and Peter Ellis, it appears, both fancied Dolly Baker, who took the part of the bat. One of Baker's understudies was Vera Hepple, who was supposed to be keen on Harold Carter. At one performance, during the duel scene between Carter and Ellis, Carter was shot and killed. Bill Darwin, who played the clown, was known to bear a grudge against Carter, and he was arrested. In the court he was proved to have threatened Carter, but he got off through lack of evidence.

"From your story it looks as if Darwin was really innocent. But wait a minute." Eadie then produced a photograph of a girl and showed it to the two men. Both recognized it as the girl they had seen firing the pistol. "Well," said Eadie, "that's Vera Hepple."

"But why should she want to kill Harold Carter, if she fancied him?" asked Harrap.

"Dunno," replied Eadie. "Could be she was rejected by Carter, and she killed him so he couldn't take up with Dolly Baker. Who knows? Anyway, I heard that Vera Hepple died around 1900 and Dolly Baker killed herself soon after. Both Darwin and Ellis were killed in the Boer War, so I don't suppose it matters much now."

Strange to tell, the ghostly actors seemed to be present whenever there was dueling or pistol play in a film. At least it was when this type of film was showing that they made their best materializations.

Situated at 317–319 Askew Road West, the Askew Picture House had an interesting site history. The buildings were erected during 1880–1882, and the premises have been occupied by a butcher, a shop, and from 1894 to 1904 a Salvation Army barracks. Thus Eadie's theater story comes from the Salvation Army days and could have been an entertainment put on by the Army. The building was demolished in 1968.

Mrs. Siddons Still Walks

Mrs. Sarah Siddons was born at Brecon, Wales, in 1755, the daughter of Roger Kemble, a provincial actor. In 1773 she married fellow-actor William Siddons, and two years later David Garrick engaged her to play Portia at Drury Lane. The role was unsuccessful, however, and she went to the provinces, where she became a firm favorite among the provincial playgoers. After a successful return to London in 1782, she eventually retired in 1812. Sarah Siddons was remembered for her tragic roles, such as Lady Macbeth.

During her period out of favor in London, Mrs. Siddons played Britain's oldest playhouse, the Theatre Royal, Bristol, which had opened in 1766. Today the Theatre Royal, Bristol, remains England's only surviving example of the larger town theater of the eighteenth century. As the oldest theater in the country, it has, with a few short breaks, been in continuous use for performances. It is recorded in the documents of the time that Sarah Siddons first played at Bath on Monday, March 15, 1779, in *The Countess of Salisbury*. That was the beginning of her "discovery," for Bristol was to be the scene of some of her greatest triumphs. So well did she do that her ghost still walks the boards and the surrounding rooms from time to time.

Actress Chili Bouchier has a personal memory of the Bristol theater phantom, which appeared to be an unhappy ghost. At the time this actress was appearing as Becky Sharpe in an adaptation of Thackeray's *Vanity Fair*. The part required one quick change, and for this Miss Bouchier used a dressing room on the opposite side of the stage to her own. During one particular performance she rushed offstage for her change to find the dressing room in darkness. She asked her dresser, a moody Irish girl, if she had switched off the light in the room, which should have been ready for the split-second change required. But the girl shook her head. The carefully arranged clothes had been disturbed, and the jewelry required by the scene had been disarranged. Discovering that one piece of jewelry was missing, Chili Bouchier sent the dresser to look for it. When the girl had left the room, the light dimmed mysteriously and the atmosphere became even colder and more gloomy. Then the actress heard, coming from the corner, the sound of someone sobbing and groaning. It stopped when the dresser came back. Questioned by Miss Bouchier, the girl admitted hearing the voice moan and seeing the lights dim on previous occasions. The room was used no more after that.

The whole theater—apart from the auditorium—was reconstructed in 1971, and since the reopening in January 1972, the specter of Sarah Siddons has been remarkably quiet. The assistant theater manager told me that the only recent interesting story is of the guard dog that refused to go into the room occupied by Chili Bouchier, or into the old fly door and wardrobe area. Barbara Leigh-Hunt, who played Sarah Siddons in *Sixty-Thousand Nights* in 1966, reports that everything went wrong for her on the opening night—wigs falling off, missed cues, fluffed lines, and so on. No such thing happened to Anne Jameson, who played Sarah Siddons in *Christmas Back in King Street*, Christmas 1972—at least she's not telling.

Taste for Music

In her book *Haunted England*, Christina Hole, the folklorist, mentions the "unknown ghost" that haunts the Theatre Royal at York. The phenomenon surrounds unexplained organ music. During the 1930's an actress and her sister, who were lodging near the theater in St. Leonard's Place, heard a few bars of "very beautiful music" around half-past two in the morning. As far as they could tell, the music came from the theater, but the streets were totally deserted at the time and the theater in total darkness. About an hour later they heard the music again. Yet subsequent inquiry the following morning did not bring to light any satisfactory explanation.

Christina Hole notes:

> I have not been able to learn what was played, or to what period the music belonged. The theater is said to stand on the site of an old monastery, only the arch of which remains, but whether this had anything to do with the mysterious sounds is not known. The actress and her sister were quite definite in their statement that they were not dreaming but

were wide awake at the time, and the fact that both of them
heard it seems to bear this out.

It is interesting to note that the organ was introduced to the
Western Church in the eighth century, which would predate
the monastery.

Mystery at Bury St. Edmunds

In psychic circles Bury St. Edmunds is famous for its ghostly
monks near the remains of the prominent abbey, which once
housed the shrine of Saint Edmund, King of the East Angles,
who was martyred by the Danes. A little-known ghost, however, is that at the Theatre Royal, Bury St. Edmunds.

Most people think that the ghost here is that of William
Wilkins, who built the theater in 1819. He is the architect best
remembered for his plans for the National Gallery in London.
Wilkins had been concerned with a theater in Bury since 1808
(when he took the lease of the little theater above the Market
Cross). His projects flourished for a time, but by 1830 he was
in financial difficulties, and the theater closed in 1843. The
theater was first called Theatre Royal when William James
Achilles Abington reopened its doors in 1845. Some say that
sorrow at his ultimate failure, or jealousy of Abington, makes
the wraith of Wilkins walk.

Rush of Cold Air at Derby

Chili Bouchier, who recorded a psychic experience at
Bristol's theater, also came across the strange happening at
Derby's Grand Theatre. She told Fred Archer, a prominent
writer of ghostly phenomena, that every time she passed the
stage to get to her dressing room, on entering the theater, she
felt a sudden rush of cold air. Her dresser too had experienced
this and told the actress that her dog cowered in fear if he was
taken anywhere near the spot.

It seems that the stage of the Grand Theatre, Derby, was the scene of at least one tragedy. Two variety artists were working on a trapeze act, when during one performance an iron clamp holding their apparatus to the stage broke loose and swung out, hitting one of the performers on the head. The girl died instantly on the stage. People remember that the "cold rush of air" was never experienced before this.

Mary Blandy's Ghost

The Kenton Theatre, Henley-on-Thames, was built in New Street in 1805 by Sampson Penley and John Jonas. It was opened on November 7, 1805, and remains the fourth-oldest theater in England. According to local tradition, the theater became inhabited in recent times by a ghost that predates the playhouse by nearly a century.

Mary Blandy was a local girl who was hanged at Oxford in 1752. It appears that she had poisoned her father for objecting to her marriage plans. From time to time, it is recorded, her ghost was seen in the garden of the house where she lived; most sightings say that she is seen under a mulberry tree, and is accompanied by the ghostly figure of her sweetheart, of whom her father had disapproved. The Joan Morgan play *The Hanging Tree*, based on Mary Blandy's crime, was staged at Kenton Theatre in 1969. During the performance, "a ghostly female was seen at the back of the stalls." It is interesting to note that a similar ghostly form was seen at Henley Town Hall, a few years earlier, when the Mary Blandy trial was being dramatized.

Phantom at the Lyric Theatre

When the game of bingo took over at the Lyric Theatre at Wellingborough, Northamptonshire, the resident ghost didn't seem to mind. This phantom has seen many changes

—that is, if one can track down which phantom it is. There are two theories. The first claims that the ghost is a disturbed spirit from an old graveyard. According to a book called *Then and Now*, published in the early 1920's by the Rev. N. Drew, there was a chapel and burial ground on the site of the theater. The Cheese Lane Congregational Chapel, as it was called, was closed down in 1903, "its graveyard was emptied and the monuments still preserved removed." It appears that the disinterred bodies were removed to London Road Cemetery in Wellingborough. Maybe, say some, the ghost is just one of the souls whose body was missed and is still buried under the Lyric Theatre. After the chapel came a leather factory. The Lyric was not built until 1936.

The second ghost theory is based on the tale that many years ago a district manager at the theater hanged himself—after the company controlling the place decided to dismantle some light fixtures of which he was extremely fond. This ghost, be it the unhappy manager or not, doesn't confine his spectral steps to the theater—he haunts the site of the former dance hall next door, not forgetting the premises of a nearby co-op.

Sightings of the ghost are well authenticated. Mrs. Barbara Mansfield, acting manager and theater secretary, told the *Evening Telegraph* on October 3, 1969:

> "I have seen the ghost, and I'm not spooky. . . . I was downstairs locking up the stockroom not long ago when I felt something behind me, and when I looked up there was something going across the balcony in the foyer—it looked like a white face. I called out: 'Who's there,' and it disappeared. I was convinced it was a trick. . . . until I saw it again, not long after."

Maintenance engineer and bingo caller Mick Lamb nearly resigned after he came face to face with the ghost one night, while working alone backstage. In the same issue of the *Telegraph*, he reported:

"I went to switch the lights on, then I went up to one of the perches and along the back of the stage to do some repairs—all of a sudden I saw it on a perch in the righthand flyer. I thought it was one of the patrons just hanging there. It scared me and I ran down the stairs, through the theatre and out into the street. I threatened to leave the theatre. I've seen it since then . . . it was in a brown jacket and possibly white trousers—a human form, but hazy."

The ghost was seen too by Mrs. Sheila LeFevre, a theater snack-bar girl, "several times when she worked in an upstairs kitchen—but now the kitchen has been transferred downstairs" (*Weeklies*, a Wellingborough publication, October 10, 1969). Mrs. Violet West, former bank clerk, with six others held a vigil and saw the ghost (*Evening Telegraph*, October 16, 1969):

"It looked like a white shadow or a statue that had been unveiled, and it moved like a jet from one side of the foyer balcony to another, and then disappeared."

An article in the *Evening Telegraph* for November 4, 1969 noted: "Now the scoffing has got to stop. A ghost really does haunt Wellingborough's Lyric Theatre." There followed a report of how members of the West Hertfordshire Psychical Research Group, and others, arranged a further all-night vigil. Television cameras, spook temperature devices, and recorders were all set up. Apparently the first to see the ghost in the balcony was Mrs. Elame Futter: "I can't really say what happened. Something just made me look up and this image was there. It was gone just as quickly as it came."

In séance manner the purported spirit was "asked questions" by one of the party. A series of clicks (one for "yes" and two for "no") was heard in answer to such queries as "Are you the spirit of someone who was alive on earth and is now dead?" Positive click. Again the questioner went through the alphabet, suggesting that the spirit of the Lyric Theatre "click" at the letters it wanted to use. The spirit is reported to have clicked at the letters H.E.L.P. Another witness saw "two red lights near us that moved slowly along the balcony and then became one. . . ."

After a rest, the spirit was asked to select more letters by the click method. The following message was received: "D.A.N.I.E.L/H.E.L.P." A further message, which was the last, was spelled out: "T.H.I.S/N.O.T/P.U.B.L.I.S.H.E.D."

Nine days later the *Evening Telegraph* reported that members of the local clergy had been asked to help "lay the spirit to rest." Subsequent messages spelled out staccato sentences for "Bless these bones" and "Bring back priest."

In a follow-up article in *Weeklies* December 12 under the title of "Soldier Returns Home—as Ghost," these comments were made:

> The ghost of Wellingborough's Lyric Theatre has appeared before, many years ago, and is well-known to old inhabitants of the town. This is the theory put forward by a brother and sister who lived in Wellingborough during their youth. They saw it on several occasions as it walked in Cheese Lane, now Commercial Lane, at the back of the Lyric Theatre. Mrs. Anne Lockwood, of 64 Cedar Way, Wellingborough, is surprised that no-one in Wellingborough has come forward before now, since so many people knew about it. Her brother, Mr. Ron Smith, of 48 Northumberland Ave., Kettering, suggests that it might be fear on the part of the local inhabitants. He explained that as children they would hide in a doorway in Cheese Lane and wait for the ghost to appear. They did this in spite of warnings never to go down there. "We saw a soldier dressed in the uniform of the 1914–1918 war. The street was made of huge cobblestones but there was absolutely no noise coming from his feet as he walked," said Mr. Smith.
>
> "As we saw the figure walk into the entry between two cottages we ran as fast as we could with the intention of

following him. When we got there he had completely disappeared," he said. They tried on several occasions and each time he had disappeared by the time they reached the entry.

Mr. Smith, who is now 49, was six years old when they first began to watch the ghost. The sombre street, lit only by a lamp bracket on the wall, the cobbled street, the limewashed stone and the haze-like figure of the ghost have all formed a heavy imprint on his memory. The back of the Lyric theatre corresponds to where the old cottages were where they used to watch the figure of the soldier. There is, therefore, more than a probability that the ghost which recently made its presence known to an experimental group in the theatre is the same one. The story became even more intriguing when Mr. Smith mentioned the legend which is attached to the ghost. Mrs. Lockwood, his sister, elucidated on the legend.

"Two brothers lived in one of the cottages with their mother and father. One of the brothers went off to war but was killed before revisiting his home. Before his death he vowed that he would return from the war."

In the early hours of November 4 this year, the spirit slowly spelled out a message to the research group in the Lyric Theatre. The words were "Daniel . . . help." Mrs. Lockwood recalled the brothers' names were Daniel and George! And so the story begins to take shape, George went off to war vowing that he would return to his birthplace. But he was killed in action and returns to Wellingborough in spirit only. He now seems to be seeking help from his brother Daniel. Mrs. Lockwood knows the family, who have since moved from the area, and she has lost track of them. She said she would not like to commit herself on the surname.

When a large sum of money was missing from the Lyric Theatre, the owners put a ban on all "after hours" psychic investigations.

Shade of Sir Henry

John Henry Brodribb, better known as Sir Henry Irving (1838–1905), made his official acting debut in London at St. James's "haunted" theater on October 6, 1866. Nearly forty years later his wraith became part of another theater's history. During April 1905 Sir Henry revived the Tennyson play *Becket* at Drury Lane, where it was enthusiastically received. This decided him to take the play on tour to the provinces. After a performance in the title role at the Theatre Royal, Manningham Lane, Bradford, Yorkshire, he collapsed and died in the foyer of the Midland Hotel. Thereafter his ghost was reported as being seen by cleaners and stagehands at the old theater.

Another Bradford theater is deemed haunted, the Alhambra Theatre at the bottom of Manchester Road. This theater has seen many famous performances, including some made by actors and actresses making their stage debuts. One such was David Hamilton, the present-day British television personality and disk jockey.

The strange occurrence happened about 7 P.M., just before Hamilton was about to go on stage. He was quite alone in his dressing room and was sitting in front of the mirror putting on his makeup. He recalls that, as he sat there, he suddenly felt odd and shivered slightly. Looking into the mirror, he saw reflected the face of a man, smiling at him. He whirled around in his seat, but the room was empty. "It was a nice smile," said Hamilton. "I could see that clearly. I knew he had not come to harm me. After the initial shock I was not afraid." Somehow, after seeing that face, the nervous tension in the pit of his stomach disappeared, leaving him with the "butterflies" which all actors must have to give a good performance.

The mystery was to deepen a few days later.

As David was leaving the theater after a performance, he was stopped at the stage door by a large group of autograph hunters. He was signing one particular girl's book, when she proudly told him that her grandfather had been an actor at the Alhambra, and showed Hamilton a faded sepia print. The face looked familiar, so David Hamilton stepped back into the doorway to examine the picture under the light. It was the face that had smiled at him in the dressing-room mirror.

Stunned, Hamilton handed the photograph back to the girl. In a moment she had hurried away with her autograph book before he had a chance to learn her grandfather's identity. Today David Hamilton is sorry that he had not had the presence of mind to find out who the actor had been—thus putting a name to the ghost at the Alhambra Theatre.

Aggie of Watford

Watford's Palace Theatre, in Hertfordshire, built in 1908 as a music hall, remains as a souvenir of Edwardian theatricals and is the home of the curious ghost known as Aggie, a friendly specter who seems to date from the time when Marie Lloyd (1870–1922), famed music-hall comedienne, graced the boards there. Most folk think that in this case the ghost is that of a former stagehand, for the spirit gets noisy if there is a lot of clutter around.

One assistant house manager and several of the stagehands have often felt Aggie's presence. Some too have heard mysterious footsteps on stage and in a particular dressing room over the scenery dock. Another incident was cited where curtains covering a door fluttered mysteriously "to one side as though someone was walking through them." This was around 3 A.M., when a set was being hurriedly erected. The team of workers watched the route of the footsteps in the gallery and were startled to see the curtains of the facing door moving as an unseen ghost passed through.

CHAPTER 7

Some European
Materializations

Glasgow Ghosts

Perhaps the most famous theater ghost in Scotland is that of the old Theatre Royal in Glasgow. There have been three theaters in Glasgow called Theatre Royal. The first and most celebrated was located in Dunlop Street. Built in 1782, it remained in use, apart from a short interval—from 1805 to 1829 a theater in Queen Street took over the name—until it was burned down in 1863. After the destruction of the Dunlop Street theater, the name was transferred to an existing theater in Cowcaddens Street, which, after two fires and subsequent restoration, became the headquarters of Scottish Television, whose employees have met a resident ghost from time to time.

It is considered unlucky to talk about the ghost, so STV employees are very reticent. However, the ghost of the Theatre Royal, it can be said, is a spirit with poltergeist tendencies—it moves small objects and replaces them elsewhere.

Before it was burned down, the Dunlop Street theater was considered the location of an animal haunting. Ross Mackintosh was a popular matinee idol of the time in Glasgow, and one morning he entered the theater and met a large yellow-colored dog on the main staircase. He threw it a piece of candy from the bag he had in his pocket. Taking no notice of the candy, the dog walked past Mackintosh and descended the stairs leading to the foyer.

Next day, in precisely the same place, the actor again saw the dog. Once more he threw the dog a piece of candy, and, as before, the dog padded past without paying it or him any attention. Thinking the actions very undoglike, Mackintosh turned around to look at the animal, but it had vanished.

Very puzzled by this, for it was not possible for the dog to have reached the bottom of the stairs in the time the actor had looked away, Mackintosh resolved to look for the dog the next day. He did so, meeting the dog in exactly the same spot. This time he threw it a piece of aniseed fudge; as the dog ignored the sweetmeat, Mackintosh tried to prod the dog with his cane. The silver-topped cane passed right through the beast, which at once faded into nothingness, leaving Ross Mackintosh feeling weak at the knees.

Apparently the dog—which had died some ten years before—had belonged to a former manager of the theater.

Dublin Ghosts

During the nineteenth century in Ireland, it became popular with managers of public houses and hotels to form parts of their premises into small concert rooms. Such an entrepreneur, Dan Lowrey, opened a house in Dublin in December 1879 called the Star of Erin. This was not a legitimate theater and only produced music-hall entertainments. It closed on February 27, 1897, and opened again some eight months later as the Empire Palace Theatre. This playhouse was to become the celebrated Olympia Theatre.

For the most part the hauntings at the Olympia take the form of noises. Lena Morgan, stage designer for Telefis Eireann (Irish Television 2), has said: "I've heard many curious tappings and bangings at the Olympia, and doors being shaken when they were very heavily chained. I have heard windows rattle, outside the room (upstairs dressing room No. 9) where I was sitting, and when I came out I realized that there was no window." The noises were heard by another theatrical/television designer, Alfo O'Reilly.

A former resident stage manager, Jeremy Swan, also attested to the manifestations of a poltergeist, which threw makeup and clothes around dressing room No. 9 during a pantomime run. "Apparently," added Swan, "there had been knocking at the door every night and nobody there." Swan once saw a glowing yellow light—from some unaccountable source—in the corridor outside the haunted dressing room; when the light passed through a doorway, the door slammed shut. Whispering noises accompanied the appearance of the knee-level light.

Tom Connor, an electrician at the theater, also heard mysterious footsteps coming down from this dressing room. He made a search but could find no one. Later he felt the theater rostrum tilt as if levitated by unseen hands.

A séance was conducted at the theater in the 1960's, and the medium Sybil Leek, who had no prior knowledge of the hauntings, noted: "I had a strong impression about the year 1916 as I stood there on the stage, and that the spirit which inhabited the theatre was of a very unruly man. It didn't belong to the theatre, yet was trapped and wanted to get out."

It transpired that the theater was the center of some violent disturbances during the Easter Uprising of 1916. A civilian—and IRA suspect—was shot on the premises by mistake. Because of the trauma surrounding his death, his spirit is deemed trapped.

The Irish actor Michael MacLiammor attests that he has heard phantom footsteps at the Gate Theatre, Dublin, but no one knows whose.

A Manifestation in Wales

The Monnow Bridge at Monmouth, Wales, has a fortified gatehouse built in 1296 for the purpose of levying toll on merchandise taken over the bridge. During the Civil War, the bridge was held alternately by the Royalists and the Parliamentarians. Today the bridge spanning the River Monnow, between Monmouth and Usk, is a curiosity, but no more curious tale is connected with it than that associated with the Richard Charles Travelling Theatre Company.

During the 1880's this company used to tour the Welsh valleys with the usual Victorian tearjerkers. Two actors in particular were with this company, Basil Hart and Harry Maynard. The company had struck some particularly bad times, and the governor, Richard Charles, had put everyone on half wages and had sacked a number of others. Harry Maynard was to be the next to go.

The traveling actors had come to Monmouth and had camped in the afternoon near Monnow Bridge. In the evening Basil and Harry were standing on the bridge contemplating whether it would be more advantageous to commit suicide than to carry on. They talked for an hour or so, and Basil excused himself, for he was on in the first play that night. Harry was not on that night; instead he had to scene-shift, but would not be needed until the second play. The two friends parted at 6 P.M.

At 7:30 the theater opened in a local hall, and Basil did well in the first play that night, getting good laughs from the audience seated on hard wooden benches. All the time he could see Harry at the back of the hall watching him. Harry was still standing, staring fixedly, throughout the three scenes of the first play, which came to a climax at 8:15 P.M. But Harry did not appear when he was due to shift scenery for the next play. He could be found nowhere.

When he had finished acting for the day, Basil searched the hall and back at the lodgings for Harry. He even went down to the bridge to look for his friend, but could not find him.

Next morning the newspaper headlines read: "Itinerant Actor Pulled out of River." "At 6:15 last night, an itinerant actor, Harry William Maynard, was pulled out of the River Monnow by the water bailiffs. It is thought that he had committed suicide."

"That can't be right," Basil said to the other shocked members of the company. "I saw Harry at the back of the hall for the start of the first play at seven thirty and again during the third scene at eight fifteen."

"You must have seen his ghost, then," offered one of the cast.

"Yes," replied Basil huskily. "Undoubtedly it was his ghost."

The Dutch Rooftop Theater

As far as is known by the Instituut voor Theaterwetenschap der Ryksuniversiteit of Utrecht, there are no haunted theaters extant in modern Holland. During the seventeenth century, however, it was fashionable for wealthy merchants to commission plays to be performed for their guests at parties or special occasions. One couple who made a living out of writing and acting in these plays were Betije and Petrus van Hooftenstalle, who converted one of their attic rooms in their Amsterdam apartment into a small intimate theater.

The van Hooftenstalles slept in bunks at one end of the theater and it was here that they began to experience strange happenings. Besides hearing unaccountable sounds—such as footsteps and voices whispering—in the theater room at all hours of the night, they would wake up suddenly to find that their bedsheets and blankets had been taken off and thrown some distance away. Further, on arriving home after playing elsewhere, they would hear someone strumming a guitar. When they entered their theater—fully expecting to encounter the instrumentalist—they found the room empty and the stringed instruments of the theater band neatly stacked as always.

One evening when Petrus was alone writing a play, he heard the sound of a woman laughing just behind him. Thinking that Betije had come home, he turned around to speak to her, but no one was there.

Perhaps the most curious thing of all was that together they experienced a dual dream. They both dreamed on the same night that they encountered a tall blond seamstress in their theater. Betije and Petrus knew she was a seamstress by her dress, and she was just leaving the theater with an antique yard measure in her hand.

"Who are you? What do you want?" they both remembered saying.

"Don't worry," the woman had replied with a curtsey. "The young man will have the best shroud I can make." With this the girl had wished them good-day and vanished. At this point the van Hooftenstalles awoke.

Struck by the oddness of having the same dream, Petrus van Hooftenstalle carefully jotted down the facts of the occurrence, with the hope that he might use them in a play.

This dream, however, occurred again and again, until one day the actor and actress came home from the market to find the girl they had seen in their dreams hurrying away from the door leading to their apartment. As they climbed the stairs, they heard the strumming of the guitar. Again the room was empty.

They told their landlady of their dream and of the unaccountable music. She recounted to them that, some years before, the apartment had been rented to a young Italian musician, whose girlfriend was a seamstress who lived nearby. One day the girl had come to her friend's apartment to find him in bed with another girl. The seamstress had killed them both as they slept. The murderess had then drowned herself in the neighboring canal. Thereafter her spirit had been seen in the apartment and the street outside.

Eventually, the ghostly disturbances in the rooftop theater

got on the van Hooftenstalles' nerves so much they did not renew their lease.

The Amorous Danish Ghost

Ludvig Holberg, Adam Gottlob Oehlenschläger, and Hans Christian Andersen were well known in Denmark for the ghosts in their plays. Few people know, however, of the ghost at the Royal Theater at Copenhagen, perhaps because the hauntings in total did not last more than two years.

Anna Christofesen was an actress at the theater during 1874–1876. One day she was sitting at the window of her dressing room when she saw a young man walk down the street. He was dressed as a thespian and wore a red flower in his lapel. Catching sight of her at the window, he blew her a kiss and disappeared into the theater below.

The young actress heard footsteps on the stairs and she turned away from the window as they stopped outside her room. A few moments later, the door of her room opened, and the young man took a step inside. She was about to let him know in no uncertain terms that she wanted none of the cheeky advances he had displayed in the street, when the giggles of some other actresses were heard down the hall, and the young man withdrew and closed the door.

Next day, as she went to her dressing room an hour or so after the midday meal to prepare for a matinee, she heard footsteps behind her in the corridor leading from the stage door. Anna turned and saw the young man with the red boutonniere a few paces behind her.

He leered amorously at her, and she was just about to give him a tongue-lashing in her native country dialect, when someone farther down the corridor spoke to her. She turned to reply to the stage manager, who had come up to her, and on reaching her room saw that the amorous young man had gone.

She didn't see him for several days. But one morning on entering her dressing room she saw the young man sitting in her armchair. Indignantly she told him to get out and leave her alone. He rose and, gathering his cape about him, left—but not before he had impudently brushed his elbow against her breasts.

Anna went straight to the manager's office in a fury and complained vehemently about the young actor, describing him in detail.

"There is no one here of that description," said the manager. "You must have made a mistake, Anna. But . . ." The manager hesitated and motioned for the young Danish actress to be seated. "What I have to tell you is strictly confidential, you understand."

Anna nodded.

"Two or three years ago, the young actor you describe was employed here. He was a lecher and wouldn't leave the girls alone. I dismissed him, and when I was paying him the wages the theater owed to him, he spat in my face and said he would haunt whoever took over his dressing room. You, Anna, are the third girl to use that dressing room who has seen him. Seen his ghost, that is—for he was killed by a jealous husband six months later."

The manager moved Anna to a different dressing room, but the hauntings continued. In time the room was not given out to actors and actresses again. It was used as a storeroom and thereafter the hauntings stopped.

The Polish Matchbox Miracle

Each year, early in December, a competition of a unique nature is held in the center of Krakow, Poland. The contest is to select the best *szopkas*, the traditional Polish puppet theaters in which miracle plays are performed. For hundreds of years, the model theaters of Krakow have given annual performances of miracle plays. It was unemployed bricklayers who made *szopkas* what they are today, for their performances enabled them to earn a few coins during the long winter evenings. Lately the *szopkas* have become a cult, but the materials for the model theaters are still simple—paper, tinfoil, and matchboxes being the most popular media.

Szopkas date back to the thirteenth century, when Polish monasteries first presented religious miracle plays in honor of the Christmas holy days. Later these plays were taken over by university students. The *szopkas* competition of 1944, however, was to be the most remarkable in living memory.

On September 1, 1939, German forces invaded Poland, and the making of *szopkas* was forbidden by the Nazis, who feared every activity that might keep alive national pride and inflame resistance. However, the traditional folkcraft was practiced in secret, and *szopkas* competitions continued.

There was an old superstition in Poland that, if the country was ever invaded, the end of the oppressor's rule would be in sight if seven *szopkas* makers sat around a *szopkas* theater in holy séance. As a mark of the truth of the oppressor's downfall, if the prizewinning *szopkas* of that year was placed on a pedestal within a circle made by the seven sitters—each holding hands to form an unbroken circle—the figures in the miracle play would come to life. At least, that is what the old folk said.

This kind of prognostication, it appears, had happened first when a monastic *szopkas* had forecast the defeat of the Mongols who overran the country in 1241. In the seventeenth century the *szopkas* of the monk Sigismund had forecast the defeat of the invading Russians, Swedes, Transylvanians, and Cossacks by the Polish hero Czarniecki. Subsequent invasions of Poland have been forecast by *szopkas* up to the early nineteenth century.

In 1944 a group of priests sat in holy séance around a *szopkas* in Warsaw. To their amazement and no little fear, the small figures of the miniature theater began to be moved by unseen hands to enact a miracle play. Would the hated Germans be swept out of Poland as the theater had indicated? Radom, Warsaw, Lodz and Krakow were all taken by the victorious armies of Zhukov and Koniev within a year.

Although the *szopkas* art flourishes today in modern Poland, divination with it is strictly forbidden by the country's Russian overlords.

Ghost at the Comédie Française

The Comédie Française, or Théâtre-Française, is the national theater of France and was founded in 1680, at the command of Louis XIV. Of all French theaters, this is the one with the best claim to be haunted, although none of the famous names of the Comédie, like Talma, Adrienne Lecouvreur, Rachel, and Mounet-Sully, are deemed to walk here in spirit form.

No, the ghost of the Comédie Française came from the outside.

Mlle. Hippolyte Clarion was a noted French actress of her day and for a time was the mistress of a wealthy Breton, M. de S. The Breton was a morose man, and his main topic of conversation was death and the supposed life beyond the grave. As his fortunes dwindled through mismanagement, he began to borrow from the actress, whom he jealously adored. This led to an embarrassing dependence of the Breton on his mistress, which led to her seeking an excuse to discontinue their association.

M. de S. bombarded the actress with impassioned pleas to return to him. She refused, even when he was reported to be seriously ill. On the night of his death Mlle. Clarion was entertaining friends to supper when, just after eleven o'clock, the company was startled to hear a loud cry, of heartbreaking sadness, outside in the street. The actress fainted with shock. So disturbed was she that friends stayed with her during the night.

The next morning the actress received the news that M. de S. had died shortly after eleven on the preceding evening.

On many succeeding nights thereafter, the cry was heard, and always when eleven o'clock had just struck. Neither friends nor police could account for the curious cry, which was now also heard—outside Mlle. Clarion's dressing-room window—at the Comédie Française.

The cries were heard nightly outside the actress's house for three months after M. de S. died; then they faded away. They were, however, easily summoned by the presence of the actress at the Comédie. Each night she appeared, the cry was heard by the audience, the staff, and the actors.

During the year of the French Dauphin's marriage to the Infanta Marie-Theresa, King Louis XV ordered that a play, in which Mlle. Clarion was playing, should be performed at the royal private theater at Versailles. Strangely, the cry of the ghost of M. de S. was heard by Mlle. Clarion and her actress friend Mme. Grandual at their lodgings at the Avenue de Saint-Claude and during the performance of the play at Versailles.

On the actress's return to Paris, the cry outside her house was replaced by a mysterious musket shot, which continued for a further three months. Then this noise was replaced by the sound of handclaps and later of music. A lovely voice singing a plaintive melody began to follow Mlle. Clarion, both in the street and at the Comédie. Two and a half years after the first despairing cry, the noise phenomena stopped completely. The period of time the noises had lasted had some significance, it seems, as was revealed long afterward.

The reason was given to Mlle. Clarion by an old lady who had attended M. de S. during his fatal illness. M. de S. had spoken of Mlle. Clarion on his deathbed, swearing that he would haunt her wherever she went, for a period as long as they had known each other. Up to the time of his death they had known each other for two and a half years.

Nikita Khrushchev's Russian Ghost

Ghost stories from the U.S.S.R. are few and far between, mainly because the Soviet Union discourages the popular discussion of psychic phenomena. During the 1950's, however, the story circulated among foreign diplomats that Nikita Khrushchev—then First Secretary of the Central Committee of the Communist Party— had seen a ghost at the famous Moscow Art Theater. Khrushchev was attending a special presentation. During the first intermission he went to the lavatory, and on his way back to his seat, he encountered a bearded man. The man was dressed in a campaign uniform of the late 1890's and on his arm was a vivacious young woman.

Khrushchev was shaken by what he had seen—his companions at the theater even asked if he had been taken ill. For he knew who the uniformed man was and could guess who the woman might be. The Soviet leader was "not himself" for many days afterward. He confided in a family friend: "Vladimir, I saw the man as clearly as I see you—a man I know to be dead. Immediately I got the security people to close the theater exits and entrances, but they found no traces of the man and woman. They just vanished.

"The occurrence rocked me to the very foundations of my beliefs," continued Khrushchev. "Next day I got my secretary to look into the State Archives. I refreshed my memory with portraits of the man—yes, it was definitely he. And as to the woman—a small, vivacious girl with a supple body, a full bosom, an arched neck, dark curls, and merry eyes—yes, it was definitely Mathilde Kschissinska of the Imperial Ballet."

Mathilde Kschissinska had been a royal mistress who had married Grand Duke Andrei at Cannes in 1921 and had later settled in Paris. At the time Khrushchev claimed to have seen her ghost, she was alive and well. Khrushchev was adamant that he had not made a mistake. The man he had seen at the theater was the archfiend of Communist mythology

—Nicholas Romanov, last Czar of All the Russias, who had been murdered with his family by the Bolsheviks in 1918.

Cheiro's New York Evil Spirit

Count Louis Hamon (died October 1936) was a world-famous palmist and seer. During his career as a psychic, he told the fortunes of most of the "personalities" of the period 1890–1920, including that of the great actress Sarah Bernhardt (1845–1923). One of his clients was the American actor James K. Hackett, who won fame for his performance in *Macbeth* in Paris, June 6, 1921. During the late 1890's, Count Louis—who was known professionally as Cheiro (pronounced "Cairo")—first met Hackett and told his fortune while they were both sitting in a railway carriage in Grand Central Station, New York. During the interview Hamon told Hackett of the "evil influences" he believed haunted the Lyceum Theater at New York City. He was never very specific, but on the occasions he had visited the theater he found it "dominated by a spirit which gives dubious gifts to its favorites." What he was suggesting was that, if the ghost liked you, then it would help your performance, but the success achieved would be a disadvantage in the long run. The ghost, it appeared, was that of a man who used to live in the building that had formerly occupied the theater's site.

Hackett ignored Hamon's advice to steer clear of the Lyceum. In a letter (to Hamon) of April 11, 1914, Hackett wrote: "When I was twenty-six, I played the *Prisoner of Zenda* in the Lyceum Theater, New York City, and the very importance of the success has artistically strangled me ever since."

A Prophesying Ghost of Rome

In 1900 Hamon was in Rome and had interviews with, among others, Pope Leo XIII (Vincenzo Gioacchino Pecci,

1810–1903) and King Umberto of Italy. During this visit the seer went on the trail of an Italian theater phantom, which he averred forecast the king's impending death.

"Can a person be sentenced to death by some premonitory warning and, despite every conceivable effort to avoid its fulfillment, finally die on the day and hour foreshadowed?" Count Hamon once asked this question at a public lecture and certainly believed such an event to be a reality. While in Paris Hamon met the actor Luigi Spartaggi, who was playing there at the time, and the actor told him a story which strengthened the belief.

One evening in the first week of January 1900, the actor had returned to his dressing room to find that someone had scrawled the name "Bresci" on his mirror. Spartaggi thought it was some kind of joke—he certainly didn't know anyone called Bresci. Again, after a performance a week later, as Spartaggi went back to his dressing room to change, he saw a woman dressed in motley coming out of the room. He called out to ask what she wanted, but she disappeared into the gloom at the end of the corridor. This time the word "Monza" had appeared on the mirror.

Spartaggi, of course, knew of the industrial and cathedral town of Monza, in Lombardy, but why should its name be written on his mirror with his grease paint? Next evening was the last straw. Spartaggi saw the woman come out of his dressing room again—what message would she leave this time? For Spartaggi was convinced that it was the woman who was doing the writing. The actor ran down the corridor after the woman, but once again she had disappeared. On the mirror was written in Italian "Remember" and the figures 1-8-7-8-1-8-7-9.

By this time Spartaggi thought it had gone beyond a joke. He went to the theater manager's office, but the manager was out. The next day, Spartaggi went again to the manager's office and, finding him there, told of the mystery writing on the mirror. The manager turned up a dusty file and showed Spartaggi that similar occurrences had happened in 1878. At the time a French actress called Viau had occupied the dressing room. She too had seen the mysterious woman coming out of the room several times. This time one word had been scrawled, namely "Victor." Days later Victor Emmanuel II, King of Sardinia and of Italy, had died.

Research had shown that, years before even Viau's time, a woman answering the description of the figure the two actors had seen had played that particular theater in Rome. Between acts she had entertained the audience with mind reading and fortune-telling. People thought that this woman's ghost had forecast the death of Victor Emmanuel II.

Yet, what of the writing on Spartaggi's mirror—"Bresci," "Monza," and the figures—what did it mean? Spartaggi puzzled it out, but could come to no logical conclusion. Then it dawned on him. If "Victor" was Victor Emmanuel, then the new writing must have something to do with King Umberto, the present Italian monarch. The fifty-six-year-old king seemed well enough. Still, a ghostly warning was a warning. Spartaggi would go to the police in the morning. They would probably laugh at him, but at least his conscience would be clear.

On his way to the theater next morning, Spartaggi bought a paper. The headlines told of the Italian king's assassination. A cold sweat of fear broke out on Spartaggi's brow. Ranieri Carlo Umberto I of Italy had been assassinated (July 29, 1900) by the anarchist G. Bresci at Monza. This time an assassin had been successful, whereas the other attempts on the king's life in 1878 and 1879 (the figures on the dressing-room mirror) had failed!

The Murdered German Actress

Baden-Baden, the German spa in the Land of Baden-Württemberg, in the Oos valley, lies forty-three miles west of Stuttgart. The mineral springs there have been known from the time of the Romans, but the great days of the spa were in the nineteenth century, when it was one of the most fashionable towns in Europe.

During one season in 1887, a group of German businessmen and their wives were watering here. One evening while they were all sitting in the lounge of a prominent Baden-Baden hotel, the conversation turned to ghosts. Most of the company expressed mild skepticism, except Herr T. A. Hoffmann and Herr Adolf Gluck. Herr Hoffman dismissed the whole subject as "utter rubbish," while Herr Gluck berated him for his "closed mind."

"There is coming to this hotel," said Herr Gluck, "a famous medium. You know of her, Hoffman—Frau Else Hensen? Now shall we engage her for a séance here at the hotel to put your agnosticism to the test?"

Hoffmann agreed.

Duly at the end of the week, Frau Hensen arrived at the Baden-Baden hotel and expressed delight at being asked to give a private sitting.

Herr Hoffman, however, was not taking the risk of being duped. He insisted on holding the séance in his suite.

"Frau Hensen," he said, "I do not wish to be made to look foolish. I believe that mediums play all kinds of optical and conjuring tricks on credulous people. To make sure that I am satisfied concerning the test, I ask you to agree to certain conditions."

Frau Hensen said that she would naturally have to hear the conditions first before she agreed.

"Very well," replied Herr Hoffmann. "First, I would require you to go with my wife into our bedroom, remove your clothes, put on a dressing gown, return here, where you must allow me to tie you into a chair and seal your secured hands with sealing wax bearing my own seal. Then, I would place your feet in a tub, half filled with plaster of Paris. When the plaster sets, I shall be satisfied that you cannot move or play tricks."

Frau Hensen thought for a moment, then said: "I agree to your conditions for the sake of my spiritualistic beliefs. But you must realize that I cannot guarantee results."

In about half an hour, Frau Hensen was tied in the oak chair, the knots were sealed with Hoffmann's signet-ring mark on wax, and her feet set in plaster of Paris above the ankles. The company of five witnesses took their place, and Herr Hoffmann locked the door to the suite, fastened the window, and sat down opposite the medium.

For some ten minutes nothing happened; all that could be heard was the medium breathing deeply. Herr Hoffmann lay back in his chair smoking a cigar, with a smile of satisfaction on his face.

Suddenly they all saw something grow from a pinhead of light, floating in the air above the medium's left shoulder. Then clearly and distinctly there appeared the form of a young woman. The head, face, and body as far as the waist became clearly materialized. Moving forward in its semisolid state, the materialization came within a few inches of a now rather disturbed Hoffmann.

"*Mein Herr,*" the female phantom said in a heavy South German accent. "Do you remember me?"

"No," replied Hoffmann. "I certainly do not."

"That grieves me, sir, although it is several years ago now. You came to my apartment in Berlin. Do you remember your Mitzi from the Imperial Theater Company? You ought to!"

Hoffmann shifted uneasily in the chair and looked askance at his wife. Against his will the former skeptic answered, "Yes, I remember now. But this must be some trick."

"No, no, it is no trick," replied the phantom actress. "Do you remember sketching me nude on my bed? We did not know at the time that my lover was behind the door curtains. He heard me say that I would come to your hotel the next day."

There was a poignant pause. Everyone held his breath.

Hoffmann broke the silence. "Look here, Gluck, must this go on?"

"You occasioned it, my friend," replied Gluck.

The ghost girl continued: "Ah, *mein Herr*, did you wonder why I did not come? Now I can tell you. I am free from all mortal silence now. I was stabbed in the belly and had my throat cut by my lover—he killed me for love of me and jealousy of you."

The apparition and the voice died away.

Herr Hoffmann wiped his forehead with a handkerchief, clearly shaken.

"This convinces me," he said, fumbling for his cigar case. "I had forgotten that episode in Berlin. Certainly none of my friends and business acquaintances knew of it. Frau Hensen certainly could not have known of it. It must be years ago —maybe ten. I saw the actress at the Imperial, and thought what a wonderful picture she would make—er—nude." He eyed his wife nervously. "I made a sketch of her at her apartment, and she said she would come to my hotel—to let me finish the picture. When she didn't turn up, I assumed she had another appointment." His hand trembled as he lighted another cigar. "I still have that sketch among my papers."

Herr Hoffmann never argued again about psychic matters. His wife was clearly not amused.

Several International Returnees

No haunted theaters are known in Sweden. And the only play the Svenska Institut at Stockholm knows of containing a ghost is *The Phantom Chariot* by Selma Lagerlöf (1858–1940). This does not mean, however, that there are no supernatural stories connected with the theater in Sweden. One story concerns an actress who died in 1913 at Stockholm while performing at the theater there. Of French extraction, the actress was a devout Roman Catholic and had required in her will that certain Masses be said for her soul. Her will, which was held by her local priest, was mislaid at the time of her death. Here is a quote from a Swedish paper of the time:

> After the death of Marie-Josephine Leclerc, the clergy of the Stockholm Catholic confraternity were troubled every night for about a year and a half by noises in their presbytery. Then the will of Madame Leclerc was found requesting ten Masses to be said for her soul. This had not been done. Immediately the Masses were said and the noises ceased. The priests associated the noises with the angry ghost of the dead actress.

Likewise, haunted theaters are unknown in Belgium, although there is a sporadic use of ghosts in the works of such as Tone Brulin, Herwig Hensen, Claude Spaak, and Georges Sim. There is this story, however, from the memoirs of Philippe Clemenceau concerning the ghost of Marie Pestanchique, who wished to repay a debt.

> In February 1899, I took over my duties of advocate. On my second week in my new office, I was visited by a woman called Claudine Fresco, who for more than a month had been in the utmost anxiety to see a lawyer. This woman stated that an actress lately dead, Marie Pestanchique, slightly known to Fresco (they lived in the same block), had appeared to her during the night for several nights, urging her to go to a lawyer. This lawyer, the specter said, would collect from her dead husband's estate fund the sum of 800 francs to pay a debt, which she, Pestanchique, owed.
>
> I made inquiries, and found that certain bills were outstanding in the actress's estate. I withdrew a sum of money and paid these off including the 800 francs stated. Subsequently Fresco was troubled no more.

CHAPTER 8

Some Psychic Puzzles

Avon Theater, Utica, New York

Some fifty years ago, it seems, a mystery woman ran down the center aisle of the Avon Theater and shot the pipe organist dead. Gossip of the time had it that the organist was cheating on his wife, and she took the traditional way out of the situation. From that time to the theater's demolition in 1947, the building was deemed haunted. Night porters at the Avon testified that the organ would rise from the pit at midnight and play music, without the assistance of human hands. The theater auditorium would be filled with this sinister music until someone entered. Then it stopped. During the last few years of its existence, the theater had difficulty employing staff, so well known did the psychic happenings become.

Piccadilly Theatre, West End, London

During the early 1970's actress Sarah Miles, who was play-ing Mary Queen of Scots in her husband's play *Vivat, Vivat Regina*, was troubled by an unaccountable "force." Miss Miles had a dazzling array of costumes to wear for the play, and for one scene she had to quick-change to a dark-red riding habit. The whole change had to be completed in around fifty sec-onds. Miss Miles' dresser, Hersey Pigot, would unbutton the garment in advance before she left the theater at night, and hang it up that way in the wardrobe in Sarah Miles's dressing room. On one particular night, when the quick change came, Pigot discovered, to her great annoyance, that the but-tons were done up. That night the change took many vital

125

seconds longer. No one in the theater knew anything about it.

The same thing happened the following night. Suspicion fell on the theater cleaners, but they all denied touching the costume. That night Hersey Pigot and Sarah Miles placed the unbuttoned dress in the wardrobe, locked it and the dressing room, and took the keys away with them. No one could have entered the room without breaking in (there were no signs of a break-in), but the dress was found the next day to be buttoned. Clearly something supernatural had taken place. The difficulties continued for a week and then ended. There has been no such trouble since.

Actress "Sees" Husband's Death in Plane Crash

American actress Jane Withers avers that she foresaw her husband's death in a plane crash. "Call it clairvoyance, intuition, sixth sense, or what you will," she says, "things have happened to me in the theater that cannot be explained any other way." The former child star says that she had a recurring dream and "intuitive flashes" when in theater dressing rooms about her husband dying in a small private plane. She only agreed to marry him when he promised to sell two airplanes he owned and flew.

"I always cautioned him not to fly in small planes," says Miss Withers. "One day, in a rush to get home from a business trip, he decided to take a private plane. It crashed and he was killed—just as I had foreseen several times."

Sometimes theater atmospheres "set off" her psychic awareness "like a force within me, a nagging feeling. It's accompanied sometimes by a tremendous illumination that almost blinds me."

Dylan Thomas at the Bush

The Welsh playwright Dylan Marlais Thomas (1914–1953) is said to haunt the Bush Theatre, London. The Bush is a small "fringe theater" that was formerly a BBC rehearsal room and is a part of the upper rooms of the Shepherds Bush Hotel. One materialization of Thomas took place in the presence of author-actor Michael Mundell and half a dozen colleagues. After a late-night rehearsal, they locked up and remembered that they had been observed by a man who had stood silently at the rear of the theater. They went back to let him out, but found no one there.

The man was subsequently described as "plump, podgy-faced, about forty, and with dark curly hair"—a description that fitted Dylan Thomas perfectly. Thomas had used the Shepherds Bush Hotel for drinking bouts after working at the BBC TV studios around the corner.

Helpful Ghosts

Mae West has long been a devotee of spiritualism, to such an extent that she began to be troubled by strange voices in the night: "Finally I had to quit fooling around with the forces, they kept me awake."

By and large, however, the ghosts around the octogenarian actress are helpful. She says she once "heard" an entire script in fifty-six seconds, "the length of the time it took to play a chorus on the piano." She dictated what she had heard from the ghost voices in forty-five minutes to her producer and director. The script resulted in "one of her best" films, *Every Day's a Holiday*. The actress reported on various occasions hearing spirit voices in a number of theaters and once she reported "a whole circle of ghost hands over my head."

City Varieties, Leeds

As recently as the 1950's this famous music-hall theater has been said to have been haunted by the ghost of a woman who some people believe is the wraith of the well-loved artist, Florrie Ford. This old theater saw the great days of music halls in the north of England, and at one time artists performed on a sawdust flooring. Florrie's Wraith, as the ghost is called, has been seen on the stage and in the orchestra pit.

Does a Famous Dead Film Star Guide Her?

Hollywood actress Leslie McRay claims that she is guided by the ghost of Clark Gable. Leslie belongs to a Hawaiian cult whose members meditate. Through this Miss McRay says she can communicate with Gable's ghost: "He inspires me and tells me every move to make."

John Brown's Voice

Another actor who is inspired by "a voice from the grave" is British actor Bill Dysart. This time the ghostly emanation is that of John Brown, the faithful Highland servant of Queen Victoria.

Dysart said that, when he was acting in the play *King Edward the Seventh*, he spoke the part of John Brown "with a voice copied from one beyond the grave." This ghost voice of the "real" John Brown was tape-recorded by a friend of Dysart at a séance held by the celebrated spiritualistic medium Leslie Flint. "It is a very hoarse voice and very much in the back of the throat." It is interesting to note that there is speculation that in life Brown was a medium and had contacted Victoria's dead husband, Prince Consort Albert.

American Actor's Incarnate Spirit

Veteran film star Glenn Ford believes that his "soul, spirit, or what you will" has lived before—as a cavalryman called Launvaux in seventeenth-century France. Ford said that he was taken by ghostly hands, during hypnotic "trips," to see his past. In vivid dreams his ghost guides showed him how Launvaux was an officer in the elite Versailles cavalry.

"Strangely enough," said Ford, "where Lanvaux was pierced by a sword, I have a birthmark that hurts at certain times." Ford also says that, throughout his acting life, he has been bothered by the ghost of a Scottish piano teacher called Charles Stewart, who was born in 1774 and died of tuberculosis in 1812. Although Ford is not a pianist, this ghost once assisted him to play, expertly, difficult works by Beethoven and Mozart when Ford was required to do this for a script.

Psychic "Prime Minister of Mirth"

The late George Robey, nicknamed Prime Minister of Mirth, delighted music-hall audiences for over sixty years. Few realized that the comedian was psychic and something of a faith healer. Successful theater producer Peter Cotes recalls an example of Robey's ready talent. During 1915, when Robey was starring in *The Bing Boys*, he was visited by Dr. Neil Collier to say good-bye before he went off to France. Everywhere he went Robey took with him a collection of charms; he gave one of them to Collier with the comment, "I *will* that nothing more shall happen to you throughout the war than that you will lose the middle finger of your left hand. Good-bye and good luck."

Dr. Collier thought no more of what Robey had said, but in 1916 during the Battle of the Somme, he "got in the way of a shell." When the smoke cleared, he found his left hand was smarting and spurting blood, and his middle finger had been blown off!

George Robey was said to haunt the Hippodrome Theatre at Manchester, but there are no modern instances of psychic phenomena connected with him.

Conrad Veidt Returns

The spirit of the German character actor Conrad Veidt is said to have returned recently to someone who worked with

him. This occurred to Mrs. Josephine Jobson of Bishop Auck-
land, County Durham, with the help of medium Betty Daw-
son of Gateshead. From Betty Dawson's description, Mrs.
Jobson recognized the actor with whom she had worked at
Denham Studios, in Buckinghamshire, in 1938. The ghost of
Veidt appeared at the séance dressed in the uniform of a
U-boat commander and wearing a monocle—his favorite role.
Conrad Veidt died in 1943.

The Haunted Jacket

Fred Archer, the journalist and psychic researcher, recounts
a strange story connected with a Victorian jacket that had
been purchased at random from a street market by a theater
property department for use in a play. The jacket, which dated
from the 1890's, was a woman's, a short-backed velvet garment in the style of a bolero. The fashion was known as a
monkey jacket—the name derived from the similar short coats
worn by Italian organ-grinders' monkeys, who used to entertain in the London streets of the time.

The jacket had been purchased for use in a play, the action
of which was the time of Queen Victoria's Diamond Jubilee
(1897). It was to be worn by the plot's hard-working seamstress, who was played by English actress Thora Hird, mother
of Broadway star Janette Scott.

When Miss Hird first put on the jacket, there seemed to be
ample room in it, but after she had worn it a while, she began
to experience an unpleasant tightness under the arms and
bodice. At first she dismissed the sensation as imagination,
but it grew worse. The unusual tightness after it had begun to
be worn was also experienced by the understudy, Erica Foyle,
and the stage manager, Marjorie Page. Miss Foyle's encounter went further, however, for when she had the jacket
on, she saw the apparition of a young woman wearing it.

The mystery of the jacket deepened when the wife of the

play's director, Frederick Piffard, put on the jacket, for red weals rose on her throat—marks such as might have been made by human fingers trying to strangle her. Others experienced difficulty in breathing while wearing the jacket.

Intrigued by the story, Fred Archer arranged a séance at the Duke of York's Theatre, St. Martin's Lane, where the play was running. Following a performance of the play, the séance was conducted in the presence of the cast, the stage manager, the director and his wife, Fred Archer, and three mediums who had been told nothing of the history of the incidents.

Here is the mediums' report:

> Medium1: No distinct psychic impressions.
>
> Medium 2: A feeling that the garment had belonged to a young woman.
>
> Medium 3: He held it for a few moments and then began to describe a dramatic vision. There was a young girl, he said, about eighteen to twenty years of age. She had a sense of guilt about something. In some way she had provoked anger akin to madness in a man who, nevertheless, was not essentially evil. The medium said he could see a pair of hands, the rough hands of a workman, tearing at the girl's clothing. The two struggled violently until suddenly the girl fell backwards and there was a splashing as she was forced into a butt of water.
>
> The assailant then dragged her body from the water and carried it up a flight of stairs into a room, squalid and bare save for two pieces of furniture. There he wrapped the body in a blanket, then carried it downstairs again, still wet and dripping. At that point the vision faded.

The comments of the latter medium were endorsed by Marjorie Page, who said that she had had a vision of similar content while wearing the jacket.

The jacket's "haunted powers" continued for some time, and the garment was later discarded by the property department.

Two Theatricals Still Walk

Oscar Fingal O'Flahertie Wills Wilde, the dramatist and poet, was born at Dublin in 1854. Today he is remembered mainly as the witty author of *Lady Windermere's Fan* (1892), *An Ideal Husband* (1895), and his masterpiece, *The Importance of Being Ernest* (1895). Wilde died in 1900, in obscurity and poverty resulting from his prosecution and conviction for homosexual practices. His ghost has been long associated with two London theaters, the Haymarket and the St. James's, where his plays were often presented.

In 1923 ghosts were seen at these theaters and spirit messages, which purported to come from Oscar Wilde, were received by actors and actresses working there. The ghostly messages were deemed genuine by the London-based Society for Psychical Research (SPR). A book was later published on the messages called *Ghost Epigrams of Oscar Wilde*.

During December 1923, two young actors and an actress held a private séance at the St. James's, and during this, it is said, automatic writing—a ghostly hand holding a pen—occurred in which the words "Pity Oscar Wilde" appeared.

This was reminiscent of automatic writing that had been produced under séance by members of the SPR, except that the latter had asked the question "If a spirit is present will you give your name?" and had received an extended answer: "I am Oscar Wilde. I have come back to let the world know that I am not dead. What you call being dead is the most boring thing in life."

Oscar Wilde's phantom pen was to write more:

> You know that we are a sort of amphibian, who has a foot in either world, but belongs properly to neither. We live in the twilight of existence. In eternal twilight I move, but I know that in the world there is day and night, seed-time and harvest and red sunset must follow the apple-green dawn. Already the May is creeping like a white mist over

lane and hedgerow, and year after year the hawthorn bears bloodred fruit after the white death of its May.

Now the mere memory of the beauty of the world is an exquisite pain. I was one of those for whom the physical world existed. I worshipped at the shrine of things seen. There was not a blood-stripe on a tulip, or a curve on a shell, or a tone of the sea but had for me its meaning and mystery and its appeal to the imagination. Others might sip the pale lees of the cup of thought, but for me the red wine of life! Pity Oscar Wilde!

To further the investigations, the SPR encouraged an additional séance to be held, in which one of the officers was present. A series of questions were asked concerning Wilde's family life. None of those present knew the answers to the questions, but later investigation proved the answers to be correct.

During this séance the SPR official asked for further evidence of the ghost's identity. The response came:

Do you doubt my identity? I am not surprised, since sometimes I doubt it myself. I have always admired the Society for Psychical Research. They are the most magnificent doubters in the world. They are never happy until they have explained away the spectre. And one suspects a genuine ghost would make them exquisitely uncomfortable.

I have sometimes thought of founding a Society of Celestial Doubters—which might be a sort of SPR among the dead. No one who left the earth under sixty would be admitted, and we would call ourselves "The Society of Supernatural Shades." One of our objects might well be to investigate the reality of . . . a psychical research worker. . . . Fortunately, there are no facts here. On earth we could scarcely escape them. . . .

There, after all, I could detach myself from my body. Here I have no body to leave off. So one of my most interesting

occupations is impossible. It is not by any means agreeable
to be a mere mind without a body.

"Will you tell me something of your prison life?" was the
next question from the SPR representative.

The ghost's answer was: "My circuit of the world's pain
would not have been complete without that supreme misery,
for to me it was supreme. I, who worshipped beauty, was
robbed not only of the chance of beholding her face, but I was
cast in on myself."

People who knew Wilde attended other séances, and theatrical experts assessed the messages of Wilde's ghost and
accredited them with the mortal Wilde's style and wit. Most
were convinced that Wilde's shade had returned to earth.

Spirit of a Film Star

British actor Leslie Howard (1890–1943) became an actor in
1917. After successes in the United States and Great Britain,
he became increasingly engaged in films and was internationally famous for his roles in *The Scarlet Pimpernel* and *Gone
with the Wind*. He was killed when the plane he was traveling
in from Madrid was shot down by German aircraft.

Some people believe that his ghost returns from time to
time. Actress Molly Weir is one. In July 1943 she said she saw
his specter just after he was killed. She remembers going to
bed on this particular night and winding up the special air-
raid blind. Sometime during the night she awoke suddenly.

"I looked toward the curtains moving slightly in the
breeze," she told friends. "Without the slightest fear I saw a
man's figure pause on the ledge a second and swing into the
room." He was smoking and Molly Weir smelled the tobacco
fumes. She recognized him as Leslie Howard. "He came toward the bed, sat down on the edge, and gazed into the
moonlight with the dreamy abstraction I'd observed so many

times in his films." For five minutes he sat there. With a sigh he stood up, moved toward the window, swung his legs over the ledge, and vanished. Next morning Molly Weir heard that the actor had been killed.

Ghostly "Actor" at St. Andrews

Playwright A. B. Paterson was undoubtedly the driving force in the establishment of a repertory company in the Fife town of St. Andrews, Scotland. Back in 1933, he and others took the lead in converting an old cowhouse into the lively Byre Theatre. Now the small intimate theater has been transformed into a new theater, which was opened in 1970.

The theater today is located between Abbey Walk and one of the medieval "lang riggs." It is here in the medieval garden at the main entrance to the theater where the ghostly "actor" patrols. This area has been a busy thoroughfare for centuries, so the wraith may date back to the days when the nearby ruined cathedral was prospering. The ghost of the Byre Theatre precinct was last seen in 1973 by an American couple, who were in St. Andrews for a golfing holiday. I interviewed them in the lounge of the Scores Hotel. Mrs. Herman Josephson spoke first:

"Herman and I had just emerged from the little passageway from South Street when we saw him. He was standing near the portico of the little theater. As I remember, he was dressed in tight trousers, white shirt, with a sort of frilly front, and leather boots. He had one foot on the steps almost as if he was reading the theater program."

"I took a few photographs," added Mr. Josephson. "And I saw him clearly through the viewfinder."

"Yes, but as we moved nearer," said Mrs. Josephson, "I could see right through him! I felt quite sick, so we went to sit down on a bench nearby."

Mr. Josephson patted his wife's hand: "When we looked

again, the man had gone. What clinched it for us was that, when we had the film developed, the man was not on the print—yet, I remember seeing him clearly in the viewfinder!"

Ghostly Warning

One morning American TV star Lucille Ball awoke feeling disturbed and depressed. It was almost as if a cloak of psychic matter had enveloped her. As she lay in bed she had the strong urge to contact her friend Helen. It was as if the psychic aura were cautioning her of some hidden danger that might affect her friend Helen and Helen's husband, Jimmy Thurston.

Helen confirmed, however, that her husband was all right. At the time he was out on some errands.

The fearful sensation would not leave Lucille Ball alone, however. "This feeling of terror still gripped me," she said. "I'd never felt anything like it before."

As she drove to work that morning, Miss Ball sensed that a terrible road accident was about to take place. This feeling of psychic doom impressed itself upon her miles before she passed the spot where police and fire vehicles had set up warning lights to redirect traffic.

On arrival at the studio, Miss Ball's sense of uneasiness pressed her to phone Helen again. "Everything's fine, Lucy," came the reply. "Jimmy's a little late getting back."

"Are you sure he's okay?" Lucy persisted.

"As far as I know . . ."

By now Lucille Ball *knew* that something had happened. She sat numbed in her dressing room. Ten minutes later the phone rang. In a very strained voice, Helen said: "Lucy—it's Jimmy! But how in God's world did you know?"

Jimmy Thurston had been killed. And Lucille Ball had been warned of the event by some kind of ghostly precognition.

Secret and Forbidden

During the eighteenth century in Europe, it was fashionable for "men about town" to become members of a Theatre of Eros. These were private theaters where lewd plays were enacted, in which members could take part in bawdy roistering with the actresses. In France the theaters were called *petites maisons*, and it was said that a former Bishop of Orléans had had such a theater in the cellars of his private palace. Certainly, Prince Philip of Orléans had a private theater performing erotic plays in Montmartre in 1749. Head and shoulders above others, however, as a patron of erotic theaters, was the Duc d'Hénin.

Plays were written for the Duc by an ex-monk called Delisle de Sales, who is still thought to walk in a house in one of the nobleman's properties in the Rue des Sts. Pères, Paris. One bookseller reported that his slumbers were regularly interrupted by ghostly footsteps on the stairs. When he went to investigate, no one was there. One night he spent an hour watching the staircase as the ghostly feet tramped up them, but no materializations were to be seen. Later the bookseller discovered an old volume that stated that his house had once been used by the Duc d'Hénin as a *petite maison* and that the phantom footsteps of past customers were often heard going up the stairs. From time to time the wraith of De Sales had been seen, too.

Dame Sybil Thorndike's Phantom Partners

When the world-famous Old Vic Theatre in London, transformed from a derelict theater by the indomitable Lilian Baylis, was closed down in 1963, Dame Sybil Thorndike commented that she was convinced that the actress's ghost was still in the theater. She had felt its presence many times.

Dame Sybil, however, has a more personal ghost, the shade

of her dead husband—the late Sir Lewis Casson. "I am always conscious of his presence," she says. The actress shared ESP gifts with her husband.

A drugstore clerk called Stephens once went to a play in which Dame Sybil was acting with her playwright brother, Russell Thorndike. Stephens distinctly saw a ghost on stage when the Thorndikes were acting a scene. Later Stephens described the ghost to Sybil, who instantly recognized it as her father, who had been an honorary canon of Rochester.

Keenan Wynn's Story

"A warning voice has been with me most of my life," says American actor Keenan Wynn. He has now learned not to ignore the warnings of the ghostly voice that echoes in his brain. Who the ghostly voice belonged to on earth he does not know, but it has been helping him since he was sixteen. It first warned him not to ride his motorcycle on a particular day years ago.

"I thought it was silly, so I did anyway. And I crashed. Since then I've raced boats and cars and soloed in planes, and have heard it many times. I'm always better off when I listen to it. Many times I have avoided bad accidents by harkening to that ghost voice.

The Contented Monk

The district of St. Bartholomew's stretches from London's Smithfield Market to the Old Bailey. Here in the twelfth century was an Augustinian priory, which was sponsored by a monk-courtier of Henry I's entourage with the strange name of Rahere. The priory was despoiled by the order of Henry VIII in the sixteenth century, but parts of the fabric were incorporated into the present church of St. Bartholomew the Great at Smithfield. The church houses the tomb of Rahere—and his ghost.

It is a well-known fact among ghost hunters that the specter of Rahere was seen by a former rector of St. Bartholomew's, the Reverend F. G. Sandwith. In fact, the clergyman saw the specter twice. Few, however, know of the encounter made by some actors in 1932 who were staging a Nativity play near the Lady Chapel. Four of them, during the final rehearsal, experienced the sense of calmness and peace that accompanies the ghost to such an extent that they looked toward the iron gates of the chapel in unison. There they saw the figure of a monk standing near the altar steps. His shadowy form faded away in the soft lights of the altar candles.

Voice from Beyond

While playing at the Coliseum Theatre in London in *Madam Butterfly*, actor-singer David Hughes told reporters that he is influenced by the ghost voice of a dead conductor. Often Hughes has heard the gruff voice of the late Sir John Barbirolli, the former conductor of the Hallé Orchestra, giving him encouraging messages and advice.

Sir Charles's Psychic Voyage

Sir Charles Henry Hawtrey (1858–1923), the actor-manager and playwright, first appeared on stage in 1881, and he became famous for producing a series of light comedies. He was interested in psychic matters and once told of a strange psychic trip that happened to him while he was playing at the Playhouse Theatre in 1920. He was not feeling too well at the time and remembered being lifted by unseen hands to a plane of astral consciousness. Of the trip he left this account:

> I was being carried swiftly through space into the upper air, on and on and on, only conscious of the most delightful feeling of exhilaration—such exhilaration as one has never even imagined.

After a while I found myself standing alone upon a gleaming pavement of black marble, a raised step in front of me, and overhead an arc of the deepest azure blue.

As I stood there I felt distinctly that I was in the presence of people who had died long before and that their ghost hands had brought me here.

In my hands I found materialised several golden balls, and these I knew I had to place upon the step in front of me. The balls were different sizes and were difficult to arrange, as they kept rolling away in all directions, so I knelt down to get at them better.

At last I did it, and those golden balls lay shining with marvellous brilliancy upon the black marble; and as I looked at them, still kneeling, I said: "I am sorry not to have done it better," and a ghost voice answered me, "Then go back and try again."

Once more I was conscious of being borne through the air, returning to earth again, and filled with the same indescribable sense of exhilaration.

Somerset Maugham commented that Sir Charles told this story many times to friends and that the incident had a profound affect on him. He believed that he had died and that for a short time had become a ghost himself. On his arrival in the world beyond he found that his life on earth had not officially ended so that he had to return—as it happened, for three more years only.

Donald Calthorpe's Story

The actor-manager Donald Calthorpe, a friend of composer Lionel Monckton, had a remarkable vision shortly before that brilliant musician died.

Calthorpe was one of a group of actors who were conversing in the Green Room, Leicester Square (where Monckton was a well-known member), when suddenly Calthorpe interrupted whoever was talking with the remark: "I believe something has happened to Lallie Monckton."

The actors knew that Monckton had been ill with influenza for a few days. Then shortly afterward Calthorpe exclaimed: "Look, look, there's his dog!"

The others looked in the direction in which Calthorpe pointed, for Monckton often brought his pet into the club with him, but they did not see anything. The time was an hour at which the composer often looked in to have a chat with his friends.

An hour or so later news came to the club that Lionel Monckton had died.

The London *Evening News* of February 20, 1924, which carried the story, sent a reporter to interview Calthorpe about the ghostly dog he had seen: "I was talking to Paul Arthur and Huntley Wright at the time," he said. "I saw the dog distinctly, but they couldn't see anything, and thought I was joking."

Ghost at the Theatre Royal, Dublin

A premonitory ghost is also associated with the Theatre Royal, Dublin, and concerns Eugène Ysaye, the famous Belgian violinist, who played the theater in 1924.

Those in the audience were aware of a sudden falling-off of Ysaye's performance at a recital given by him and Dame Clara Butt. When Ysaye left the stage, he told some friends that he had had a ghostly premonition of a fatality that had happened to someone close to him. 'I saw this wraith on stage," he said. "It pointed to me and, as if it talked in my mind, told me not to grieve but that someone dear to me had passed from this earth. I continued to play, but the soul had gone out of my music."

Ysaye went back to his hotel and there found a telegram awaiting him saying that his wife was seriously ill in Brussels. Five minutes later came another cable to say she was dead.

A Ghost on Location

According to psychic writer Jack Hallam, the ghost of Lulu von Herkomer, wife of the Baron Herkomer, is said to haunt Bushey Film Studios in Hertfordshire, England.

Baron Herkomer's country mansion was demolished to make way for the studios. Before the mansion went, however, there was the history of hauntings by a ghost called Lulu. Annoyed at being disturbed, perhaps, the ghost Lulu made her presence known while the first film was being shot here. According to one actor, "a luminous blue lady stalked through the unlit gloom of a set, frightening two young actresses and scaring a producer out of his wits."

Actor Victor Maddern remembers a haunting in more recent times. Maddern had occasion to spend a few nights in one of the dressing rooms at Bushey, only a few feet away from the old path trodden by Lulu the ghost. Victor Maddern passed two uncanny nights in the complete silence of the deserted studio; on the third night he could stand the silence no longer and fled to the parking lot to sleep in his car. "I'd just settled down," he recalls, "when there was the most horrible shriek I have ever heard. Definitely not human."

Miss Fanny's New Theatre

In the London Guildhall Library, there is a picture called "The Cock Lane Uproar," with the subtitle "At Miss Fanny's New Theatre in Cock Lane." The illustration concerns perhaps London's most famous ghost, the poltergeist of Cock Lane, which attracted the attention and comments of such notables as Dr. Samuel Johnson and Oliver Goldsmith. The story is included in this collection because it was considered in its day "the best piece of theatrical work of the season."

The ghostly trouble began in January 1762, and, as usual, the first news of the sensation appeared in London's periodical press. Within hours the literary hacks were producing "plays" about the story for the capital's teeming burlesque reviews.

The story began simply enough.

In 1757, one William Kent married an Elizabeth Lynes of Lytham in Norfolk. Within twelve months she died in childbirth, and her sister Frances—or Fanny—moved in to keep house for her brother-in-law. Unable to marry—the law did not permit a man to wed his deceased wife's sister—Fanny became William Kent's mistress, and thereafter they lived as man and wife.

Ultimately they moved to lodge with Richard Parsons at 20 Cock Lane, near Giltspur Street, Smithfield, behind St. Sepulchre's Church, Snow Hill, where Parsons was officiating clerk. Parsons had a daughter Elizabeth, aged eleven years, who was to become the central figure in the ghost story.

On one occasion, William Kent had to leave London, and not wishing to sleep alone, Fanny asked Elizabeth to share her bed. This occurred for a night or two, until one morning Fanny complained to her landlady, Mrs. Parsons, that she and Elizabeth had been roused from sleep quite often by bumps on the ceiling, scratchings on the bedposts, and rappings under the bed and in various other parts of the room. Mrs. Parsons told Fanny that a cobbler next door sometimes worked nights and that he could have been responsible for the "manifestations." Fanny was indignant when the noises continued. As one play put it:

> FANNY. Pray does your shoemaker work hard on Sunday nights as well, madam?
> MRS. PARSONS. Nay, mistress, that he does not. So what can them noises be?

To the devotee of ghosts, "them noises" seem to be a classic case of a poltergeist haunting. And people began to say that the manifestations were the admonitions of the ghost of Kent's wife for Fanny's cohabiting with her sister's former husband.

Fanny was terrified. In her country way, she imagined that she was about to die. She soon did die.

William Kent, it seemed, had lent his landlord a sum of money, which was not returned. A court case ensued, and Kent and Fanny found new lodgings at Bartlett Court, Red Lion Street, Clerkenwell. Here Fanny died on the evening of February 2, 1760, of smallpox. It began to be whispered that she was killed by thoughts of the "ghost" that had haunted her at Cock Lane.

A lull occurred thereafter in the "ghost's activities" at 20 Cock Lane. Then in early January 1762, the disturbances started once more—again around the bed of Elizabeth Parsons. The knowledgeable said that the child was the focus of "poltergeist activities," and Richard Parsons took her both to a clergyman and an apothecary for opinions, but to no avail. As in all classic cases, the poltergeist followed Elizabeth from her own house to those of her neighbors. Eventually, wherever she went, the child was followed by the elite of London society. "It was as if Betty Parson's bedroom was a theater," one broadsheet commented. Séances by the dozens were held at the haunted house in Cock Lane, attended by the Duke of York, Lady Mary Coke, Horace Walpole (a Member of Parliament), and many others. Sometimes up to fifty people crowded into the room, lighted by the light of one candle, to gape at the bed of the child "to whom the ghost comes."

The ghostly rappings and scratchings at Cock Lane continued, and eventually a nurse, Mary Frazer, suggested that the noises might be messages in code. By accepting one rap for "yes" and two raps for "no," Parsons purported to question "the entity" and therein deduced that the new disturbances were caused by the ghost of Fanny, who claimed that her death had been caused by red arsenic being put in a draft of ale for her by her "husband," William Kent. Later the ghost added that she "wanted to see William Kent hanged."

It was also stated in the popular press that Elizabeth saw a shrouded figure standing by the bed, without hands; other witnesses said they saw "luminous apparitions," with hands.

Cock Lane's ghost became a cult and plays based on the case's content were sponsored by David Garrick and others and ran at the Haymarket Theatre and other houses.

Maybe there were originally some genuine supernatural phenomena in the Cock Lane house, but some deception was discovered, and the principals involved in them were tried before Lord Chief Justice Mansfield. Parsons was sentenced to the pillory and prison, his wife and others involved were imprisoned. It is thought that Parsons used the "original phenomena" to "get even with Kent" for suing him for the unrepaid money. The whole truth about the Cock Lane Ghost will never be known.

The Phantom Baritone

Wolfgang Amadeus Mozart (1756–1791), the great Austrian composer, believed in ghosts. Some believers in psychic phenomena have credited Mozart with conjuring up a "ghost voice" to assist actor-singer Raimund Herincx.

Raimund Herincx once played the role of the Spanish grandee, Count Almaviva, in Mozart's *The Marriage of Figaro*. As he heard the Covent Garden orchestra begin the introduction to *Vedro, mentr'io sospiro*, he filled his lungs. But as he was about to hit the first note his voice failed. In a moment of panic Herincx prayed for help. He felt the stage darken, and he became very sleepy. Then just as he began to experience a cool draft of air, he heard a rich baritone voice, more resonant than his own, singing his lines. During this, too, Herincx saw the ethereal form of his long-dead singing teacher smiling at him from the wings. After what seemed a few seconds, Herincx "woke up" in his dressing room, having no recollection of performing in the rest of the opera.

Herincx subsequently admitted that he has had supernatural assistance on stage several times.

The Phantom Head

Charles Hollis, the actor, once told journalist Stanbury Thomson of some gruesome phenomena he encountered when on tour at Shrewsbury, England. His company had taken rooms at an old Tudor mansion for rehearsals and their overnight stops.

Said Mr. Hollis: "One evening, as it was beginning to get dark, a very strange thing happened. We had just finished rehearsals, had had supper, and were about to retire. That night, I must tell you," explained the old actor seriously, "there seemed to be a kind of strange uncanny influence hovering about us, as if someone of an undesirable character were present.

"However, fighting against this terrible fear, we mounted the spiral staircase and made our way to our rooms. Of course, this old manor still retained its original polished oak floor and old wainscot paneling. Believe me, it gave us a strange morbid impression of the dark ages of our forefathers. Well, to continue with the story, we were startled on entering the room by a sudden clash like that of swords, and to our horror a head rolled across the floor. A head, with black piercing eyes bulging from their sockets, with flowing locks similar to those grown in the reign of the first King Charles [i.e., 1625–1649]. Of course, the ghastly head vanished, and we did likewise as soon as we could, fully determined not to stay at old places again as long as we lived."

The American Actor at Cherbourg

A strange story was told to me a number of years ago, while traveling through France in a train. The story concerned an

American actor-scriptwriter called Peter J. Hone, who died a mysterious death.

Around 1935, Peter J. Hone had been commissioned by an American university to make a written study of theaters in France. As this would need extensive travel in France, Hone had taken a ship from New York to Southampton and thence to Cherbourg. He happened to spend a night at the Auberge Parnasse, a small tavern in the town of Cherbourg, for the purpose of breaking his journey to Paris. Hone arrived at the little inn before sunset with all his bags and was soon shown to his room by the landlord, a little hump-backed Frenchman, standing about five feet tall and as ugly as any gargoyle. The room was small, but clean and comfortable, and Hone had a welcome shave and wash before joining the rest of the guests at dinner.

During the meal the only one to whom Hone could talk was the humpbacked innkeeper, Pierre Deschoses, as the rest of the guests were Dutch and German. Hone's maternal grand-mother had been French, and he spoke the language with fluency. Hone spoke for about an hour with the innkeeper, accepted a drink or two, and retired to bed about midnight. Being very tired, he was soon asleep.

Around four o'clock in the morning he was awakened by a queer noise, a kind of mumbling, muttering, and droning—in fact, a kind of hideous noise. The background noise went on for some time, until Hone got really annoyed. Jumping out of bed, he listened to where it was coming from. It seemed to be downstairs, but where? Casually gazing out of the tiny paned window of his bedroom, he noticed a ray of light thrown onto the path that led up to the side door of the inn. Hone realized that the light was coming from the kitchen window.

The kitchen light made Hone feel hungry, and putting on his dressing gown, he went down to see if he could get a sandwich from whoever was still awake.

Hone found the kitchen after a while and quietly walked in

without knocking. There he saw one of the strangest sights he had ever seen. Sitting at one of the working surfaces on a high stool was the dwarf Deschoses, almost caressing a pile of money, bills and coins. He quietly picked up handfuls of coins and put them back and patted thick rolls of banknotes. He counted and recounted with giggles of unrepressed delight.

Somehow Hone lost the feeling of hunger, but found that his hands were beginning to itch at the sight of the money. He watched the deformed Frenchman carefully put the silver money into a tin box and this and the bills into a battered suitcase. Watching all the time from behind a huge cupboard, Hone saw the innkeeper click the case shut and move over to a private staircase, which presumably led from the kitchen to the old man's private apartment. On the third stair Deschoses stopped and, leaning forward, removed the fifth wooden step. With an avaricious grin the little man slid the case out of sight and restored the step. Then, rubbing his hands with a kind of nervous excitement, the innkeeper went on up the stairs to his room.

Peter J. Hone began to think as he had never thought before. There must have been about ten thousand dollars in that case, if his judgment of the bills had been correct. What he could do with that money! Back in America he wouldn't have to play third-rate theaters, or write scripts that no one wanted to read. He made a plan.

First he went back to his room to pack his things. On returning to the kitchen, he thumbed through a French railway guide at the deserted reception desk and saw that there was a train to Paris in half an hour. He could be away and safe in the capital before the money was missed. In Paris, he could change the money bit by bit into American dollars and then, wowweee!

Carefully Hone counted the wooden steps and, putting his fingers under the rim of the fifth, pushed upward. But the step would not move. Hone strained his fingers painfully, but could not make the step move. It must have a secret bolt. He looked around the kitchen and, taking a meat-ax from a hook on the chef's table, he began to insert the blade under the step. Slowly the wood began to creak upward. Finally it split to reveal the suitcase. He had no sooner grasped for the case than he looked up to see the terrible perspiring face of the innkeeper, looking down at him from the top of the staircase.

"Que faites-vous là avec cette valise?" shouted the innkeeper.

Hone had gone too far already. He bounded up the stairs and before he really realized it, he had grabbed the innkeeper by the throat and was throttling the life out of him. Hone saw the little man turn red in the face and then a sort of blue color. His eyes bulged from their sockets and the man collapsed into Hone's arms, quite dead.

In a space of an hour Hone had gone from a tired, quiet actor to a thief and a murderer.

Panicking, Hone picked up the innkeeper's body and, running into the inn's courtyard, hid the corpse in a garbage can. Quickly Hone returned to the kitchen to collect the money and his bags. In ten more minutes he was on the train for Paris.

Formerly a healthy man, Hone began to feel very nervous about his actions. He could neither eat nor sleep. From a Paris doctor he got some medicine to help his appetite and a draft to help him sleep, but they had little effect. Wherever he went, he began to hear the jingle of money and saw with increasing intensity images of the dead innkeeper—images on walls, on furniture, and, worse, on the back of his eyelids as he slept. Hone continued his work visiting theaters and libraries, but as he looked up from books, from plates in a restaurant, or from the windows of buses, he would see the figure of the innkeeper watching him. As he sat alone in his hotel room, smoking in an armchair in the evening, the innkeeper was bound to be sitting opposite, emerging from a sort of white ectoplasmic mass.

A devout Roman Catholic, Hone regularly went to Mass and

found temporary comfort in that. Yet there were times when Hone was nearly at his wits' end. He wept, he prayed, he pleaded, but he could not get rid of the—he now knew it to be the ghost—image of the innkeeper ever watching him. One night Hone could stand it no more and ran around his hotel room ranting and raving and screaming, "God curse the damned innkeeper and his money." He poured glasses of brandy down his gullet and smoked endless cigarettes. At last the booze calmed him a bit.

He sank into a chair.

All at once a gentle tap came on the door. Having no response, it echoed again. Hone staggered to the door, seized the knob, and opened it. He froze, for there in the hallway stood the figure of the innkeeper, looking at him exactly as when he had discovered Hone stealing.

"Pierre Hone, I have come for my money," said the innkeeper in his guttural French. "I have come for my gold. Get it at once." He held out a long transparent hand toward Hone. As Hone was rooted to the spot, the ghost said the same again, but added, "I have come for my gold—and you."

Hone now found that he could move and retreated into the room. He knelt near the bed and pulled the innkeeper's suitcase from under the draperies. Placing the suitcase on the table, Hone took a few steps away from it and watched the innkeeper nervously. The little man—Hone could see the rest of the room clearly through his body—picked up the case and disappeared with it out of the door.

A few minutes later Hone felt better than he had felt for weeks, and putting on his hat and coat, he went to evening service at the Cathedral of Nôtre Dame. After the service he approached one of the priests and asked for a private interview. During this he recounted in every detail his murder of the innkeeper, his theft, and his ghostly visitor. The priest advised him to go to the police and Hone left.

Next morning the body of Hone was found, clutching a hymn sheet from the evening service, in a garbage can in a side street of the Quai de l'Hôtel de Ville near the cathedral.

Today the case is still an open file in the archives of the Paris Sûreté. The priest to whom Hone had spoken was found, and as Hone did not tell the priest the story of the innkeeper under the seal of the confessional, the priest gave the police details of the little man's murder. The police and the priest could only speculate how Hone had died, but, curiously, the dead American actor's neck showed distinct signs that he had been throttled.

The Case of the Hog-Faced Lady

Some years ago an actor and his family lived in a house in London's Blackfriars district. The house has now been demolished. When the actor lived there, he was charged only a small rent, because no one would live there long. Desperate for a place to live, the actor took up tenancy and asked no questions.

"One night," said the actor to friends at Covent Garden one day, "as we were about to retire and had reached the foot of the staircase leading to our bedroom, my wife and I heard footsteps on the landing above us. Both my wife and I were aghast. 'Oh, no, we've got burglars!' I gasped. But no. A rustling of a lady's gown followed. Then the air seemed to go chilly and cold. Death seemed to be hovering about in its most terrible form. The footsteps became clearer, and there appeared before our eyes, at the top of the stairs, a lady in an old-fashioned dress—I should say probably early seventeenth century. Then she began to descend the stairs. Strange to say," the actor explained, "she had the head of a pig, an ugly, repulsive pig—small eyes and snout complete. Well, down this horrible creature came—moving toward us. My wife screamed and then fainted. I managed to catch her as she fell. Looking up, my wife still in my arms, I observed with great pleasure that the terrible thing had vanished."

The actor, William Barrett, told this to a playwright friend, who within days made a remarkable discovery while researching in the library of the British Museum. He came across a torn, dusty pamphlet published in London in 1641, bearing the title "A Certain Relation of the Hog-faced Gentlewoman."

The gist of the story was as follows:

> The pig-faced lady, whose name is Tamakin Skinker, was born at Wirkham on the Rhine, in 1618. Some people assume she is English-born, being a native of Windsor on the Thames. All the limbs and lineaments on her body is well featured and proportioned, only her face, which is the ornament and beauty of all the rest, has the nose of a hog or swine; which is not only a stain and blemish, but a deformed ugliness making all the rest loathsome, contemptible, and odious to all that look upon her. Her language is only the hoggish Dutch "ough, ough," or the French "owee, owee." Forty thousand pounds is the sum offered to the man who will consent to marry her. Her person is most delicately formed; and of the greatest symmetry. Her manners are, in general, simple and unoffending, but when she is in want of food, she articulates, certainly something like the sound of pigs when eating, may perhaps be a little disagreeable. Miss Skinker is always dressed well. She is now in London looking for a husband. She lives——Blackfriars or Covent Garden. The doubt between the two places is lest the multitude of people who would flock to see her, might, in their eagerness, pull the house down in which she resides.

It appears that Miss Skinker also appeared at taverns and theaters trying to get herself a husband. But there is no record of her wraith at Covent Garden where she once appeared.

Bibliography

Archer, Fred, *Ghost Writer*. London: W. H. Allen, 1972.

———. *Ghosts, Witches & Murder*. London: W. H. Allen, 1972.

Baird, A. T., *One Hundred Cases of Survival after Death*. London: T. Werner Laurie, 1943.

Bardens, Denis, *Ghosts and Hauntings*. London: Zeus Press, 1965.

Barker, Kathleen, *The Theatre Royal, Bristol*. Bristol, Eng.: Bristol Historical Association, 1969.

Bligh, Neville M., *The Story of the Theatre Royal Drury Lane*. London: Theatre Royal, Drury Lane, 1969.

Braddock, Joseph, *Haunted Houses*. London: B.T. Batsford Ltd., 1956.

Clarke, Cumberland, *Shakespeare and the Supernatural*. London: Williams & Norgate, 1931.

Clarke, G. E., *Historic Margate*. Margate, Kent, Eng.: Margate Public Libraries, 1972.

Clarke, Ida Clyde, *Men That Wouldn't Stay Dead*. London: John Long, 1936.

Day, James Wentworth, *A Ghost Hunter's Game Book*. London: Frederick Muller, 1958.

Girvan, Ian, and Margaret Royal, *True Stories of the Ghosts of Bath*. Bath, Eng.: printed privately, 1974.

Grant, Douglas, *The Cock Lane Ghost*. London: Macmillan & Co., 1965.

Green, Celia, and Charles McCreery, *Apparitions*. London: Hamish Hamilton, 1975.

Hallam, Jack, *Ghosts of London*. London: Wolfe Publishing Ltd., 1975.

Hole, Christina, *Haunted England*. London: B. T. Batsford Ltd., 1940.

Holzer, Hans, *The Lively Ghosts of Ireland*. London: Wolfe Publishing Ltd., 1968.

Hopkins, R. Thurston, *Ghosts Over England*. London: Meridian Books, 1953.

Huggett, Richard, *Supernatural on Stage*. New York: Taplinger Inc., 1975.

Moro, Peter, and Brian Little, *The Story of the Theatre Royal, Bristol*. Bristol, Eng.: Trustees of the Theatre Royal, 1971.

Owen, George, and Victor Sims, *Science and the Spook*. London: Dennis Dobson, 1971.

Price, Harry, *Poltergeist over England*. London: Country Life Ltd., 1945.

Sargeant, H., *A History of Porstmouth Theatres*. Portsmouth, Eng.: Portsmouth Papers XIII, Portsmouth City Archives, 1971.

Statham, Margaret, *The Theatre Royal Bury St. Edmunds*. Bury St. Edmunds: printed privately, 1965.

Stead, William T., *Real Ghost Stories*. New York: George H. Doran, 1921.

Steiger, Brad, *Strange Powers of ESP*. London/Australia: Scripts Publications, 1970.

Stevens, William Oliver, *Unbidden Guests*. London: George Allen & Unwin, Ltd., 1946.

Thompson, Stanbury, *Ghost Stories*. London: Arthur Stockwell, 1948.

Underwood, Peter, *Gazetteer of British Ghosts*. London: Souvenir Press, 1971.

———. *Haunted London*. London: Harrap, 1973.